Donated by

Jerry Zimmerman
2012

AMERICAN
VISA

DATE DUE

DEMCO 38-296

AMERICAN VISA

SHORT STORIES BY
WANG PING

COFFEE HOUSE PRESS
MINNEAPOLIS ☞ 1994

Book design and cover art by Nora Koch

Cover calligraphy by Qian Shao Wu

Back cover photograph by Rudy Burkhardt

The publishers would like to thank the following funders for assistance that helped make this book possible: The National Endowment for the Arts, a federal agency; The Jerome Foundation; The McKnight Foundation; Dayton Hudson Foundation on behalf of Dayton's and Target Stores; The General Mills Foundation; Cowles Media Company/Star Tribune; The Andrew W. Mellon Foundation; and The Lannan Foundation. This activity is made possible in part by a grant provided by the Minnesota State Arts Board, through an appropriation by the Minnesota State Legislature. Major new marketing initiatives have been made possible by the Lila Wallace–Reader's Digest Literary Publishers Marketing Development Program, funded through a grant to the Council of Literary Magazines and Presses.

Coffee House Press books are available to the trade through our primary distributor, Consortium Book Sales & Distribution, 1045 Westgate Drive, Saint Paul, MN 55114. Our books are also available through all major library distributors and jobbers, and through most small press distributors, including Bookpeople, Inland, and Small Press Distribution. For personal orders, catalogs, or other information, write to:

Coffee House Press
27 North Fourth Street, Suite 400, Minneapolis, MN 55401

Library of Congress CIP Data
Wang, Ping, 1957–
     American visa: short stories / by Wang Ping.
          p.   cm.
     ISBN 1-56689-025-X (pbk. : acid-free)
     1. Title
PS3573.A4769A8 1994
813´.54—dc2   94-12599
                                                              CIP

Printed in Canada

Table of Contents

To my mother and grandmas

LIPSTICK

In some deep corner of the dinner table, I found an old lipstick.

The cover was gone, its green plastic body coated with dark greasy dirt. I wiped it with a tablecloth and held it under my nose. I smelled the fragrance of wild roses. Slowly I turned the tube as far as it could go. About an inch of scarlet red appeared between my fingers. The print of someone's lips on the top, its angle so tender that I dare not touch it. Whose lipstick could it be? Who still had the guts to keep a lipstick in 1971, the prime time of the Cultural Revolution? Anything which was related to beauty, whether Western or Oriental, had been banned. Gray *zhongshanzhuang*—Mao's suit—became the uniform for the middle-aged and old people, and the green and navy blue uniforms became young people's most desirable objects. All the woman had short hair cut just below their ears. Some girls tied their hair with rubber bands into two brushlike pigtails. They were called revolutionary brushes because they resembled the brushes people used to write critical big-character posters.

Whose lipstick could it be? My sister Sea Cloud's or my mother's? Sea Cloud's power seemed limitless. Although she was only twelve, and was two years younger than me, she was three inches taller—five foot, five inches—and looked like my older sister. In fact she had me completely under her thumb. She made me do her share of the housework, which was only one-third of the work I had to do. Her excuse was that I had no friends to see and no places to go to anyway. She made me tell her a story every evening. If I refused, she pinched and cursed me as my mother did: *dead ghost, wooden-head, abacus.* Sometimes when the pinch was too painful and I grabbed her wrists, she would holler for my mother. My mother always punished me with the bamboo stick behind the door. She said that since I was the oldest daughter, I should love and take care of my younger sisters and brother. I had two sisters and one brother. Fortunately, my youngest sister stayed with my grandma in Shanghai, and my brother was not as wily as Sea Cloud. Everyone said Sea Cloud looked exactly like my mother: big double-lidded eyes, long clean eyebrows, straight delicate nose, and clear white skin. She looked like a foreigner, people also said, with admiration in their voices.

I couldn't understand why Western books and ideas were poisonous but to look foreign was desirable. Whenever I couldn't bring any food from the food market or broke a bowl or burnt rice, my mother would sigh: If only you were half as smart as Sea Cloud. I talked back in my heart: If only she could do her own homework.

Every Chinese New Year, my mother killed one of the chickens I raised and made chicken broth. She asked me to bring a bowl of chicken soup to Sea Cloud, who was always sick in bed with a stomach ache or a bad sore throat just when every hand was needed for the holiday preparations. I hated Chinese New Year. It meant endless washing of dishes and vegetables in cold water and listening with an empty stomach to guests feasting and laughing. I slowly dried my swollen frost-bitten hands on my apron, staring at the hot chicken soup with hatred. I'd been washing dishes piled up to my chest from nine to three o'clock. My mother said, "Don't pull a long face. You should love your sister and take care of her. She's sick." As soon as my mother turned her back, I spat into the soup and stirred it with my greasy finger. Then I brought it to Sea Cloud with a big smile.

The lipstick. My sister wouldn't have hidden it inside the table. She had her own steel box with a lock on it. If it had been hers, she would have shown it off long ago.

Then it must be one of Mother's old belongings. Somehow it had escaped the Red Guards' confiscations in the fall of 1967 and had been lying in the table since then. The dinner table was the only piece of furniture that survived the confiscation. All other pieces were taken away or burnt, together with books. It was an eight-fairy table made of *nanmu* wood, square, with heavily decorated legs and edges, and a drawer on each side. The drawers were no longer there. The vacated space was perfect for hiding my books. As long as I kept them in the center, no one could reach them. Only my thin arm could get through the six-inch-wide and two-and-a-half-inch-high drawer space.

Today was my lucky day. At fourteen and a half, I had my first lipstick.

There was some dust on top of the lipstick. I wiped it on the ball of my left thumb, the only spot on my hands not covered with frostbite scars. The bright red mark startled me and the slightly sticky lipstick on my skin sent an unspeakable sensation along my arm to my scalp. I trembled as I rubbed the lipstick mark on my hand. I was remembering a scene in my childhood.

☞

I was five years old, a senior in the Navy Boarding Kindergarten. That night we were going to give a performance in the Navy Auditorium. My parents would come to the show. I hadn't seen them for two weeks. The weekend before, my father's ship was on duty in the East China Sea, and my mother was too sick to take me home. I was too excited to nap, so I stole into the playroom. The teacher forgot to lock the closet where the costumes for the performance were stored. I picked up the general's hat with its shiny beads and two long striped whips sticking out on each side. Since I'd be singing behind the curtain with the chorus, the teacher said I didn't need to wear any costume. I tried on the hat. As I was looking for a mirror, I found a basket with some lovely round boxes and tubes in it. I opened one of them. Rouge. How beautiful the pink color was! The teacher said she'd put the makeup on for us after dinner. This must be it. I lifted the pad and rubbed it on my cheeks. I wished my parents could see me. I wished I had a mirror. Someone grabbed my pigtail and pulled me out of the closet. It was the teacher. She yelled and shook me like a madwoman. "You smelly beauty, you little bourgeoisie! Just like your mother." Her screaming was so loud and piercing that soon I couldn't hear anything, although her mouth was still opening and closing like a stranded fish on the beach. She dragged me into the room where twenty other children were napping and walked me around. I must have looked strange with that general's hat on and rouge all over my face. The children laughed and called in chorus: *smelly beauty, smelly beauty.*

I was taken out of the performance and delivered to my parents that night.

I rubbed some lipstick from the ball of my thumb onto the back of my hand, its scarlet red thinned and faded into pink, like the color that always glowed so splendidly on my sister's cheeks. Whenever I saw her, I'd pray with an aching heart: Oh God, please give me beauty like Sea Cloud! But I remained the ugliest in the family. My eyes were small and my eyelids were single-layered; my eyebrows short and thick; my nose bony and too big on my small face. Whenever we had a fight, my sister would call me "small-eyed devil." I was pathetically thin and pale. My mother sometimes ground her teeth in anger and told me that I deliberately made myself skinny so that I could make the neighbors pity me and accuse her of maltreatment.

I looked at my rosy hand, hoping for a miracle.

It was nine o'clock. I had three hours to perform this experiment, find my book, and cook before mother came back for lunch. Little by little I lifted the table from the floor. I was actually looking for a book that I'd hidden in the table the night before. I'd pushed it inside in a hurry and pretended to study English when I heard Mother's footsteps. Its title was *Deep Is the Night*, written in semi-ancient Chinese about a woman warrior disguised as a man who somehow remained pure among the lustful and corrupt men. After the five-year ban, books were very hard to get. The bookstores had only Mao's books on their shelves. I'd secretly been trading books at school through a well-organized underground book network. Everyone obeyed its strict rules: Never betray the person you got the book from; never delay returning books; never re-lend without the owner's permission; pay back with three books if you lose a book. I owned some very good books: *Grimm's Fairy Tales, The Blossom of Bitter Herb*, and some Russian spy novels. I had torn off the covers and wrapped them with the red plastic covers for Mao's works. I traded for books about herbs, medicine, stars and constellations, and of course, I cherished novels. Once I got a porno book about monks and nuns digging tunnels between their temples to meet at night. Something called *Burning the Red Lotus Temple*. My sister caught me reading it in the public bathroom and threatened to tell on me unless I let her read it. I had no other choice but to give it to her. She wasn't as skillful as me in terms of keeping books away from my parents. Maybe she just thought they wouldn't punish her. My father caught her and hit her for the first time. He hit her so hard that he broke the handle of the broom. The book was thrown into the stove; my sister had to write three self-criticism papers and read them in the family training class my father organized. To my surprise, my sister, who had told on me and gotten me in trouble with my mother many times in the past, took the punishment alone with heroic silence. I really admired her for being such a good sport, and I willingly gave up three of my best books to my friend as a compensation for the lousy porno book.

I straightened the table, locked the door, and stood in front of the mirror on the wardrobe door in my parents' room. I looked at myself in despair. My features were still as bad as they were a month ago—white patches of fungus and strips of peeling skin on my dark face, the result of the strong liniment my father had applied to my face to cure the fungus. He had believed that my face was infected with athlete's foot. My jacket—passed down from my grandma to my mother, then from my mother to me—was splotched with dirt on its shredded sleeves, patched elbows, and front. I looked pathetic. I was pathetic. I'd graduated from high school two months ago, the youngest graduate, with straight As in every subject. Still I couldn't go to college. Universities were open only to peasants, workers, soldiers, and the students who had received reeducation for more than two years in the countryside, factories, or army. Nor could I get a job in town. Factories and other businesses had stopped hiring people since the Cultural Revolution started; they could hardly give the salaries to their old employees. No one worked, no one was allowed to work. Making revolution was more important than production. My only choice was to go to the countryside to receive reeducation from the poor and middle-class peasants. I was willing to go. After two or three years, I might have a chance to be recommended to college. But Mother said I was too young. She wanted me to stay home to grow fat and learn some English. The truth was she wanted a free maid. Since graduating in February, I had taken over all the housework, cleaning, washing, shopping for daily food, and cooking. My mother didn't have to do anything except sit down for meals and take naps at noon. It was my mother who grew fat. I got thinner and paler.

The lipstick was the only bright color in the room. Everything else was gray or brown—my face, the walls, the furniture, the sheets. I held it up to my mouth. It brightened my face.

I applied it to my lips. The first touch was frightening. I practically jumped as the lipstick left the first red mark on my lips. It was like being kissed. I laughed at the idea. How much did I know about kissing? I'd never been kissed on the lips or anywhere else. My mother never touched me except when she knocked on my head with her knuckles. Not that I wanted her to touch me anyway. I put some lipstick on the ball of my thumb and rubbed it on my cheekbones. Then I turned to the mirror.

The figure in the mirror was grotesque, with her scarlet lips and uneven red rouge over white patches of fungus on dirty cheeks, the tube of lipstick between her chapped, stained fingers. The effect was like a rose in cow dung. I pushed the mirror away. There was no miracle. Was I destined to be a housemaid all my life?

I poured some hot water into my mother's basin and washed my face. No one must see any trace of lipstick on me. As I rubbed my cheeks, rolls of dirt came off. I hadn't been to the public bathhouse the whole winter. I took off my clothes and soaked my mother's washcloth in the water, breathing in the warm comforting steam. Little by little I cleaned myself, from my face to my legs, until the water in the basin turned black. Then I picked the coal out of my nails and the folds of my knuckles with my mother's toothbrush. Yesterday I made coal balls from coal powder for the stove. It was cheaper than buying them. Mother said we must be more economical since we had an idler at home, meaning me of course. I opened mother's bottle of vaseline on the dresser and applied some to my face and hands.

Finally I took hold of my braids. They were the only thing on which the neighbors ever complimented me. Thick and glowing with bluish darkness, they hung loosely down to my waist and swayed as I walked. It was almost a miracle that I still had them. Long braids, together with curly hair and colorful clothing, were considered the tails of capitalism at the beginning of the Cultural Revolution. I still remembered how the Red Guards patrolled the streets with scissors in hand and jumped at passersby who were wearing tight pants or had long hair. After they cut open the legs of the pants or cut off the braids, the victims had to recite Mao's words and express their sincere gratitude to the Red Guards for saving them from the horrors of capitalism. Although things had quieted down a lot, my long hair could still bring me trouble. My parents also hated my hair. My father thought it was dirty. Whenever he picked out a long hair from the food I cooked, he'd stare at me and roar, "Cut it off tonight!" My mother kept telling me my hair sucked all the nutrition out of my body. "You look like a ghost with long untidy hair," she screamed with her beautiful voice. Slowly I unbraided my hair and brushed it with my mother's hairbrush. It worked much better than my little plastic comb. My hair was so thick even my mother's brush couldn't get through it.

When I turned back to the mirror, I saw a different person. She was clean, had shapely lips, a slender neck, long legs, and breasts that were firm like pigeons' bellies. I turned to see my back. Once my mother measured my hips to make me a pair of shorts. After the measuring, she pinched my behind and said, "You have a big ass." My big ass looked fine in the mirror. It traced a smooth curve below my waist. I raised my arms, holding two handfuls of hair. It looked like the wings of some powerful black bird in the sunshine. Tears filled my eyes. I wasn't going to be ugly all my life.

I wrapped the lipstick in a piece of white paper and put it back into the dinner table. No one else except me could reach into that two-and-a-half-inch-high, six-inch-wide drawer. I had an hour to clean my mother's towel, hairbrush, and toothbrush, and to cook lunch. Today's menu was fish, pickles with sliced pork, sprouts, and seaweed soup.

REVENGE

⌒ "Are you going to do it or not, Seaweed?" Mother asked when I set the egg-drop soup on the table, the last course for lunch.

I pretended that I didn't hear her, my face expressionless—a strategy for avoiding an unpleasant confrontation or unwanted questions. I stared at the three dishes I had prepared: the yellow croaker had only a skeleton left, its shrunken white eye gazing up from the collapsed socket. My sister had just picked the last piece of sliced pork from the sprouts with her chopsticks and dropped it into her wide-opened mouth. The only food left on the table was pickles with sliced potatoes and the bowl of sea-weed egg-drop soup. I avoided my mother's eyes. Everyone in this Navy compound, including her enemies, agreed that her almond-shaped eyes were charming, even bewitching. To me, however, they were like a sharp kitchen knife that could chop me into shredded pork at any moment.

"Well, what's so hard to make up your mind?" Mother's voice was now full of irritation. "Don't tell me you still care about that *sha bi* after she insulted your mother and sent her brother to beat you and your sisters? Do I have to repeat the name she called me, do I, eh?"

I flinched at the words *sha bi*—silly cunt. It embarrassed me more than anything to hear Mother cursing like a shrew. Why couldn't she act the same at home as she did at school and other places—elegant, witty, and pleasant?

"Let's talk about it after the meal," Father intervened. "Not good for your digestion to get angry when you eat." Although he was smiling, I could see the frown hidden by his eyebrows. I wished that he had the guts to tell Mother to stop using stupid words in front of the children and stop bugging me like this. I was also glad he didn't. It would only cause another quarrel, which always ended with dishes smashed, table and chairs overturned, and Father apologizing. Besides, *bi* was also Father's favorite curse.

"You don't see it, old man. I'm afraid your daughter cares about that slut more than her mother. No, I can't have it. That *sha bi* called me *CHO BI.* How dare she? Nobody calls me 'stinky cunt,' nobody!" Mother pounded her bare chest with her fists. In summer, she wore nothing above her waist but a bra so that she could sweat freely.

"And she called me *lao bi,*" said Nainai, my paternal grandma, her wrinkles deepened with indignation. My brother Haihu, Sea Tiger, tittered. Nainai gave him a stern look. "It's not funny, Tiger. That woman has no respect for elders. I'm more than old enough to be her mother, and she called me 'old cunt?' I say, Seaweed, time for you to grow up and help your family. You'll be fifteen after the Spring Festival, really a big girl. That woman has gone too far. I know you like her. But does she like you? She beat you up. She insulted not only your mother and me, but also your father."

"Mother, can't we finish our lunch in peace?" Father frowned, this time without disguise. "Sit down and eat, Seaweed. Next time, please cook faster so you can eat with us. Have some soup, Mother, and you, too." He handed his wife and mother each a bowl of soup. "Eat and take a good nap. We'll have a family meeting this evening and settle the matter."

Mother and Nainai became quiet and puckered up their lips to blow on the hot soup. They never listened to him except when he pleaded for a harmonious meal. Often he would suddenly drop his chopsticks to look around the table proudly, squeeze Mother, and pat every child on the head, saying, "This is my family, my family." Oh, it was so embarrassing—more even than my mother's bra—that I wanted to climb under the table to avoid his tap.

Soon the soup was all consumed and everybody went to bed. I quickly cleaned the table, fed what was left over to the chickens, washed the dishes, and curled up in the corner of the bed I shared with my two sisters, Sea Cloud and Sea Gull. Sea Gull was visiting us that summer. Mother had sent her to Shanghai to live with Waipo, our maternal grandma, when she was two years old, because Mother didn't have enough energy to take care of four kids and work at the same time. Once a year, she traveled to Shanghai to visit Waipo and Sea Gull. But this year, she decided that Sea Gull should come to Dinghai and stay with her "real" family for a while to get to know her parents and siblings. When she arrived in a white satin dress and red leather shoes, I saw Sea Cloud's eyes glisten with envy and jealousy. She immediately invited her youngest sister to play hide-and-seek with us in the yard, but Sea Gull declined politely, saying that she didn't want to mess up the dress *da yi*, our first aunt, had bought her for her birthday. Sea Cloud was pissed off. Did she think she had three eyes or two noses? Was she something special? Apparently not. But how come she got to live with Waipo and wear fancy clothing? What right did she have to act so arrogant? "No one must talk to Sea Gull," she ordered.

As I observeded the forlorn look on Sea Gull's face, I felt sympathy for her. Mother had also given me to Waipo a few months after I was born. Until I came to live with my parents on this island, at the age of four, I had thought Waipo was my mother. The separation from her was harsh, but I gradually learned to forget Shanghai and Waipo's comfortable bed. My sympathy withered, however, as I felt Sea Cloud's anger. She was right. How come Sea Gull got to return to Shanghai after a short visit whereas we had to stay on this shabby, muddy island with nothing but stinky fish and gray Navy soldiers? The clever Sea Gull soon realized her mistake. She reconciled with the "leader"—Sea Cloud—by offering her the chocolate bar she had brought from Shanghai. They soon became inseparable.

I lay in bed with my back to Nainai. She had been sitting on her bed, her legs crossed and her hands in her lap, following my movements with her sharp, beady eyes, waiting for the moment when our eyes would meet so she could start a conversation about revenge. I was determined not to give her the opportunity. I couldn't do it.

For three days, my mother and Nainai had been pressing me to avenge myself and my family honor on Aunt Young. They laid out all the reasons that I should do it. First, it was my duty as the eldest daughter to obey the adults and carry out certain things they couldn't do. Obviously, my father's position in the Navy didn't allow him to beat up a woman. And my mother, just released from the three-week training class for the royalists and rightists at her school, still had to attend weekly meetings to receive criticism and make self-criticism. My *nainai* was old and crippled by her bound feet. My two sisters and brother were too young. Although I was going to be fifteen, legally I was still a child, and couldn't be punished. What could my school do to me—cut my salary, demote my rank, shut me up in a training class? Nonsense! Second, I need not be intimidated by Sha Bi.

Yes, she was wider, but I was taller. Yes, she was twenty-two years older, but I was stronger. Who in this Navy compound could carry fifty *jin* of rice and potatoes and walk three miles like me? No one! All I had to do was pull her stupid pigtails and knock her down. My two sisters and brother would jump on her and teach her a good lesson.

Ah, if it were as easy as my mother predicted! Aunt Young, Aunt Young, I called her name silently, that was the silliest thing you had ever done.

She used to be my mother's best friend. Of course her name wasn't Sha Bi at that time. My mother called her Little Young, and the kids called her Aunt Young. They were regarded as a pair of beauties in the Navy compound, my mother as the Western type—tall, big-eyed and high-nosed—and Young as the Oriental type—small, plump, and delicate like a doll. The only difference was that my mother was much more respected for her vocation as a teacher and her talent at singing and playing musical instruments, whereas Young worked as a clerk recording furniture borrowed and returned by Navy families. The way she dressed was a favorite topic of gossip among the neighbors. Look at her two braids, women sneered at her back, doesn't she realize she's almost thirty-seven, a mother of two children? And look at the shirt. Pink lace, how ridiculous! She and her husband had the same last name and similar features. People suspected they were relatives, cousins, maybe even brother and sister. "Nonsense," Mother yelled when I told her the rumor. "When husband and wife love each other, they begin to look alike."

Most women disliked her because their husbands always compared them to her. Why couldn't they do their hair and dress as neatly as Little Young? Why couldn't they treat their husbands with as much affection as she did? Why? the women complained to each other. Because they didn't want to suck their husbands dry like that fox spirit did. Just look at Captain Young. Whenever he returned home from the sea, he would lose weight and become pale. Fortunately, he came home every two months and stayed only two weeks. She followed him everywhere, even holding his hand on the streets. How disgusting! How could their husbands expect them to do the same?

Even my parents thought she was a bit too much. One day, they came over to play cards. Uncle Young complained about his backache and dizziness. Father said, "You must have overdone it. You know—the 'chamber affair.'" Young and his wife blushed like sixth graders. My mother immediately yelled at us and threw us out of the room. My sister kept bugging me to explain the 'chamber affair' until I got impatient and told her to ask Aunt Young herself since she was her pet.

It was about a year ago that she got her nickname Sha Bi. Her husband's ship had been away for more than seven months. Whenever she visited my mother, she would complain about her headaches and insomnia. Mother always advised her to take some sleeping pills or to see an herbalist. After she left, Mother turned to Father. "She's very horny. She'll sleep with any man. Don't you dare go near her."

Mother was right. The next day, Father came home with a mysterious smile and pulled Mother into their bedroom. My sister and I listened behind the door. Aunt Young was caught sleeping with a clerk in her office. The poor man was only nineteen years old. Apparently she had seduced him. They had been closing their office door quite often recently and aroused suspicion. That day, they shut themselves in the room again. When their colleagues kicked the door open, Young barely had time to pull her pants up. They said she had a smashingly white ass. "What a pity! She and the young clerk are finished," Father said.

Young's husband couldn't bear the humiliation and asked to be sent to the South China Sea to train new soldiers for a year.

That aroused more indignation in the treacherous wife. Young was completely isolated. Except for going to work, she shut herself up in her apartment, staring out of the broken window repaired with white strips of paper. The night she heard her husband wasn't coming home, she smashed the window with her fist. For weeks she walked around with her bandaged hand like a miserable ghost. Women and children began to call her Sha Bi.

Sea Cloud used to visit her frequently. Young called her "princess" and stuffed her with presents: a hair bow, an embroidered handkerchief, a badge of Mao with special designs, all the little silly things my sister treasured and showed off from time to time. Young often told Mother, half joking and half serious, that she would like Sea Cloud to be her *gan nuer*—her goddaughter—or her daughter-in-law. Since the scandal, Mother forbade Sea Cloud to visit Young. One day, someone informed her that Sea Cloud had entered Young's apartment. Mother immediately sent me over to check. I was ugly and dumb and immune from Young's corruption.

I knocked and was told to enter. She was sitting alone on the bed, soaking her feet in hot water. Standing at the door, I quickly glanced around her bedroom. This was the first time I'd been invited in. All her furniture was light brown, the curtain and bed sheets pink, but everything seemed to be fading away under the dust. Young looked white, as if all the blood had drained out of her. Only the feet in water were pink and tender. She lifted one foot and dried it carefully with a cream towel.

"I came for my sister," I said.

"I know. She's not here. Won't you sit down? You've grown again, Seaweed." She stared hard at me through the steam rising from the basin.

I sat down on a stool in front of her. The skin on her legs and feet was incredibly smooth. Mother had a great body and face, but her legs were always covered with red goosebumps like the skin of a scalded chicken.

"Feet have to be dried thoroughly or they'll get moldy. I can't stand athlete's foot. Do you have it?"

I nodded in embarrassment. I got it from the towel I shared with Grandma.

"What a pity. You must be careful not to let it spread over your body, especially your private parts. I assume you wash that area daily?"

I blushed. No wonder people called her *sha bi*. Should I leave, I wondered? But what she had said was fascinating. Nobody had ever discussed their private parts with me.

"And I assume you use separate basins and towels?" she asked me very seriously. Seeing me shaking my head, she exclaimed, "Oh, no, Seaweed, you don't want to get athlete's foot in your private parts, do you? Separate the basins and towels immediately. Whenever you touch your feet, you should wash your hands with soap."

"Even at midnight, when I'm asleep?" I often woke up scratching my itchy feet.

"Even at midnight."

I nodded while wondering if I had the discipline to get up at night and wash my hands every time I touched my feet.

"You're going to be fifteen, right?" She looked at me thoughtfully. "Have you had your first period yet? Your father was really worried about you last time he talked to me about it. He asked me if you should be checked by a doctor."

My father was also a *sha bi*, I thought angrily. Why and when did he talk to her about my period? What was going on between them?

"Nothing to worry about, Seaweed." Young's voice had never sounded so tender and attentive. "I didn't have my period till I was seventeen. We're just late bloomers. Do you know you're actually quite pretty? Of course, it's not the same kind of beauty as your sister's. You're the classical type, very rare nowadays. Don't be embarrassed. Have you gone out with any boy yet? No? Soon you will. Don't let him squeeze your breasts too early. If you can't resist, make sure he touches both of them at the same time; otherwise they'll grow into different sizes. How's your mother? Does Chi still come to see her every day? Oo-la-la, he's a handsome boy. Your mother has good taste in men. Do you have to leave? Come back. I'll braid your hair, French braid. I guarantee you'll look better than Sea Cloud."

I ran out laughing. Her nonsense was so embarrassing, yet so fascinating. The next day, after much debating with myself, I went again to see her. I wanted to hear again that I wasn't ugly, that I could even look better than my sister. My secret visits continued until the fight broke out three days ago.

Actually it had nothing to do with me. Young's daughter Ying and my sister quarreled over a ball on the playground. Sea Cloud called Ying her mother's nickname and all the other kids laughed. Ying ran home cursing and crying. In a few minutes, she came back with a bottle in her hand, kicked our apartment door open, and threw it in. The bottle hit my parents' wedding picture on the wall and exploded. The contents of the bottle—chicken shit and dirt—splattered all over my parents' bed, together with broken glass and their wedding picture. She jumped up and down hysterically, her face smeared with tears, screaming at the top of her lungs, "Your mother is a *chou bi!* Your mother is a *chou bi!*"

"Oh my, oh my!" Nainai rushed out from the kitchen. "Ying, isn't your mouth a bit too dirty? Your mother taught you that?"

Ying leapt at her wildly. "You're a *lao bi, lao bi, lao bi.*"

I was too shocked to say anything. Sea Cloud responded

much faster. She pulled Ying's collar, slapped her face, then shouted word by word: "Your mother is Sha Bi."

Ying ran home again. We began to clean up the mess. Fortunately it was Sunday afternoon. My mother went out to a movie with her friend after lunch. My father stayed at the dining table with his liquor bottle and drank himself into a stupor. I was shaking the dirt and shit off the sheet outside the door when Ying returned with a bearded man.

"Uncle, this is her sister." She pointed at me.

The man stepped forward and knocked me down. Before I realized what was going on, he had already kicked me into a ditch. Sea Cloud ran out and screamed, "What are you doing to my sister?" Then she tumbled into the ditch, right on top of me. Sea Tiger woke up from his nap and ran out to watch the fun. He was shoved in as well.

I turned over in bed. Nainai was still sitting in her bed, looking in my direction. I closed my eyes quickly before she opened her mouth. She had been watching me like this for three days. They wouldn't let me go unless I beat up Young for them. Yes, for them. I still couldn't believe she had sicced her brother on me. It was Sea Cloud who had called her names and slapped her. He had mistaken me for Sea Cloud. I was the victim. It was up to me to decide if the revenge was necessary. What right did Mother and Nainai have to force me like this? If they were so eager to defend the family honor, why didn't they beat her up themselves? But did I have the guts to disobey my mother? How long could I endure her grinding voice and the searchlight of my grandma's beady eyes? And the reproaching silence of my sisters and brother? They hadn't talked to me for three days, as if I were Young's ally.

At dusk, Mother rushed home from school and directly into the kitchen where I was sautéing snails on the coal stove. "He's gone," she said, her face flushed with excitement. "The brother, back to Shanghai with Sha Bi's son. I saw them boarding the ship and her wiping her tears. Now you'll have only two to deal with—Sha Bi and her daughter. Just you alone can beat them flat. No more hesitation, I tell you. I want it done today. Let's move up our family meeting since we're all here."

She glanced at her husband, her mother-in-law, and her four children. "Sha Bi is on her way home. I want you four kids to wait at the door. When she appears in the yard, Seaweed will run out and knock her down. All you have to do is hold her hands. Your sisters and brother will do the rest. Sea Cloud, you should use the long rolling pin, the one we use to make noodles. Sea Tiger, go find the wash stick behind the door. Sea Gull, take this." Mother handed her six-year-old daughter the bamboo stick she used to punish us. Sea Gull brandished the weapon in the air, imitating the way mother hit us. Everyone laughed hilariously except for me.

"Seaweed, give the spatula to Grandma and get ready. Did you hear me? Stop sautéing the snails and listen to me!"

I held the spatula in the air. The snails hissed inside their shells with helpless anger.

"Seaweed," Father called gently, "you're a good girl. Please help your mother this time? You know, we let you finish high school though it was a waste of time and money, and giving up the job in the military factory is really a great sacrifice to the family. But we understood you and supported you. Now it's your turn to help us."

I waited till the last drop of sauce was boiled dry and poured a cup of cold water on the snails. The hot wok sizzled. I banged the cover and said, "Get ready."

Everything took place exactly as Mother had arranged except for one little detail. As soon as Young rode into the yard on her bike, I dashed toward her. She got off the bike and stood obediently like a little schoolgirl expecting her teacher. We stared at each other for a second. Her hair was so black and her face so pale. I reached for her braid and she collapsed on the ground, no resisting, no crying for help. I didn't even have to hold her hands as Mother had told me, but I did anyway. How soft her hands were, and how slippery! Just like the raw snails. Suddenly I had the urge to break the shell and see the inside. See the famous white ass. "Watch out, Seaweed!" my sister shouted. I looked up. Young's daughter Ying was charging toward me, a red brick lifted above her head. The madness in her eyes spurred me on. I pulled down her mother's pants.

I still remember the loud cry from each window of the Navy compound when I exposed Young's snow-white ass. Everyone shouted at the same time as if one person. Then, the dead silence. Ying froze with the brick above her head. I suddenly lost all my courage and fled, followed by my sisters and brother.

Eight months passed by quickly. I was anxiously counting the approaching date of the pledge ceremony at which I would officially be admitted into the Youth League of Dinghai Middle School, where I had graduated the year before. I had handed in at least ten application letters and had been doing volunteer work in the school chalk factory like a lunatic to show my determination: arriving early every morning to start the machine, set the modes, and produce the bulletin news, staying late to clean up. On Sundays, I walked miles with a group of volunteer students to the Navy base to wash sheets for soldiers. I wanted to become a member of the Youth League so badly, not because it was a great honor, a step toward joining the Communist Party—the highest achievement in one's political life— I wasn't that ambitious, but because I needed to belong to something, to be recognized somewhere. Since the fight, my neighbors avoided me as if I were a monster. That was nothing compared to the silent treatment my family gave me. My sister and brother no longer asked me to tell them stories or help them with homework. My mother and grandma talked to me only to give me chores or scold me. Even my father seemed to ignore me. It made me feel as if I were invisible, nonexistent, totally annihilated. I was often seized by the horrible thought, as I chopped vegetables at home or packaged chalk in the factory, that this was all I would do for the rest of my life: chopping and packaging. Rather die than live a life like this, I told myself. Time to leave. It didn't matter where, as long as I got out of this apartment, this factory, and this island. There was nothing to hold me here anymore.

When my advisor, Huang, my former teacher of political science, finally gave me the admission form to fill out, he congratulated me and told me that the Youth League unit of the school factory had agreed unanimously that I was a perfect candidate. All I had to do now was to relax and wait for the pledge day. His assurance, however, made me more anxious and suspicious. Things couldn't go so well, not for me. I must prepare myself for the worst.

The day before the ceremony, he came with a puzzled face and took me out to the school pond. I leaned on the weeping willow. It was the same spot where Teacher Huang had told me the devastating news, on my graduation day, that I wasn't qualified for the college entrance exams unless I had worked in a factory or on a farm, or served in the army for two years. What was he going to tell me this time? If it was bad news, why here? I respected him and was grateful to him; he was the only teacher in school who had shown real concern for me. He had encouraged me to study for the entrance exams. It had also been his idea that I volunteer in the school factory in order to join the Youth League. He had given me hope—would he also destroy it?

"I know you're a strong girl, Seaweed," he said, avoiding my eyes, "But I still don't know how to tell you."

"The Youth League, right? I'm not going to be accepted, right?" I asked ferociously.

"You worked hard. But someone said that your motives weren't pure enough."

"What is it really? At least I deserve the truth." I managed to control my voice and tears.

"All right, it's the woman from your Navy compound. She went directly to the principal and accused him of admitting a hoodlum into the Youth League. She showed the pictures of her injury and the hospital bills. I was shocked, you know, and wouldn't believe it. You've always been gentle and modest. Anyway, if you hadn't pulled down her pants, things might have been different. I wish I could help you. If you want to cry, I can understand."

Somehow I felt relieved, as if someone had pulled out the cork that had been clogging my throat ever since I beat up Young. At this moment, I realized how little I cared about the Youth League. I had paid my debt. I no longer owed anything to Young. Now that I was free, I must think about what to do next. I had to change my life.

"Teacher Huang," I turned to him calmly, "I want to stay here by myself for a while. You must have tons of things to do. So why don't you leave first?"

He seemed both relieved and disappointed that I wasn't crying. Suddenly he looked worried. "I don't think it's a good idea to hang around here by yourself. It's getting late. Don't you have to go home to cook supper today?"

I laughed, baring my sharp white teeth. My diligence was known throughout the school. But there would be no more diligent Seaweed. No more humble Haizao. Today, at least this moment, I was not afraid.

Huang was startled and stepped back when I grabbed his hand. "Good-bye, Teacher Huang," I said in a loud, cheerful voice. "Don't worry about me. I'm not cooking today. Remember, my name is Haizao—the strong, solid seaweed."

And I sat on the bank of the pond till evening came. I made the decision that I would go to the countryside as an "educated youth" and work my way up to college. I was going to pick the poorest village where no other "educated youth" wanted to go so that I would have no competition when the village and the people's commune leaders recommended me for school.

LISHAO
VILLAGE

The sun was setting behind the Lightening Mountain. Along the stream flowing down the eastern mountain came the peasants from the rice fields. They departed at the village entrance and hurried home. Women had two suppers to cook, one for their husband and children, the other for the pigs. And before it got dark, the men worked on their *ziliudi*—the strips of land the government had allowed them to keep for growing vegetables when their land was turned over to the people's communes in the fifties. I leaned against the stone gate, watching them disappear down the small lanes. I was too tired to move another step; besides, I was in no hurry to go home. I'd been in Lishao Village for three months and sixteen days. Work in the fields was hard, much harder than I had imagined and prepared for. Twelve hours a day, seven days a week, in the blazing sun or cold rain. I had stopped thinking of the difference between weekdays and weekends since the peasants worked 365 days a year except for days of heavy rain and the Spring Festival. What terrified me most, however, were the leeches. They clung to my legs and sucked blood until their bodies bulged like bottles of soy sauce and couldn't hang there anymore. The first time I saw them on my ankles, I screamed and threw up.

The cool stone felt good on my back and arms. I narrowed my eyes to watch the sun sinking inch by inch. Its last fiery rays dyed the Lightening Mountain and Lishao Village a golden orange. I stretched out my hand to peek at the sun through my fingers. My hand became golden orange, too. A huge wave of solitude overwhelmed me, the solitude that had haunted my childhood and adolescence. How many times at dusk, when everything changed colors, had I hidden in a corner or behind a door or a tree, weeping, imagining my own death, and feeling homesick at home?

Homesick? I shook my head. Even in my most exhausted moment, I'd never regretted or doubted my decision to come to this village. The feeling of liberation since I left home was so exhilarating that I had been transformed into a completely different person. I could curse in the filthiest language that would make even the toughest peasants blush. I could strip a young man's pants for a bet of fifty fen. The villagers had already nicknamed me Crazy Weed. I smiled as I imagined how Mother's eyes would pop out if she witnessed my behavior. I had been considered the most obedient girl in the neighborhood, though quite dumb and ugly.

Burning itches on my arms. Blisters from the sun. I scratched hard. Yellow juice oozed out. Pain. But it was worth it. Think about two years later, when I would be qualified to be recommended to colleges. I would rather kill myself than live a life like my parents: working, eating, sleeping, gossiping, quarreling for money, and growing old. No! my life would be different. It would be full of meaning and beauty. I would have the best education, best work, best love, and best family. My children would never ever weep behind a door or a tree!

I put my fingers in my mouth and made a long whistle. Excited quacking and chuckling came from the yard of my house. Hong Hong appeared first, her wings flapping up and down to accelerate her speed. She was followed by Yaya, her round body rolling from side to side to catch up with Hong Hong.

I had brought them from home. Mother was going to kill them for dinner. She was angry with Hong Hong because the hen hadn't laid a single egg since she was purchased from the market a year ago. Mother had recently bought the duck, hoping it would soon lay eggs, but it just squat in the corner of the cage and refused to eat.

"Can I have them, Mother?" I asked. I had brought her a basket of fresh bayberries as a present on my first visit home. It was her favorite fruit. I could tell she was very pleased. "I have a lot of space and food in the country, maybe they'll lay eggs there. If you kill them now, you can't get much meat out of them. They're so skinny."

Mother shrugged her shoulders and put down her knife.

Two weeks later, Yaya laid her first egg at night in the stove. She had become a handsome duck, with smooth, golden brown feathers. Hong Hong was sick for a long time. She wouldn't eat, her stomach swelled up like a rock. Sitting next to the stove, she hiccuped and shook her head violently as if she had to get rid of something from inside her body. I didn't know what to do. My friend Young Su came over, examined her, and said that she probably had a ball of hair tangled with food in her gizzard. The only way to save her was to open her stomach and get it out.

I watched Hong Hong a long time that night. She was dying slowly. Why not give it a try? I tied her feet to a chopstick, pulled the feathers off her stomach, and cut it open with a razor. A ball of black hair, mingled with sand, grass, and rice, filled the whole gizzard. No wonder she couldn't swallow any food. After I cleaned her stomach, I sewed it back together with a needle and thread. That night Hong Hong slept in my bed.

Hong Hong had laid fifteen eggs since then. I pickled hers, and Yaya's, in salt water.

We went home together, Hong Hong perched on my left shoulder and Yaya on my right. Our home was in an old one-story house near the village entrance shared by three families. Before I came, the peasants had divided the room into two so that I could have a kitchen as well as a bedroom. They had also built a stove near the only window and a dining table near the wall. My bedroom had a skylight, a desk, a stool, and a bed that consisted of a plank and two benches. For the room and furniture, the village received two hundred yuan as an "educated youth settlement fee" from the government.

We walked into our home. The door was ajar. I left it that way so that Hong Hong could use my bed to lay her eggs. She wouldn't do it anywhere else. The hen and duck jumped off my shoulders onto the stove. It was a single wok stove, with a tin bucket buried next to it. Whenever I cooked, the water in the bucket would also be heated for drinking or washing—a good way to save fuel. I lifted the cover. A layer of rust appeared at the bottom. Again I forgot to dry the wok thoroughly and grease it with lard. I cooked only every other day. In the beginning, I tried to cook four meals a day as the peasants did—breakfast, lunch, dim sum, and supper—but, I found it impossible. We had only about half an hour for lunch break and twenty minutes for the afternoon dim sum, including walking back and forth between the fields and home. I didn't know how the other peasants managed to swallow two or three bowls of rice (always hot, as they believed cold food was harmful) within such a short time. For me, there wasn't even time enough to

light the stove. I would either be late or I'd go back to the fields
with an empty stomach. Finally, I started making a lot of rice in
the evening and eating the leftovers for lunch and dim sum.

I stored the rice in a bamboo basket and hung it on a hook
attached to the ceiling. This was the only way to keep mice
away. There were many of them, especially at night, always
busy with their gnawing, squeaking, scurrying, and fighting.
Two had fallen from the ceiling into my water jar. I didn't dis-
cover their bodies until I tasted the foul smell in the water and
started cleaning the bottom of the jar. The sight of the decom-
posed mice and the thought of having drunk so much bad
water turned my stomach. But the next morning, I drank from
the jar just like always. I congratulated myself on becoming
tough. In fact, I had gotten so used to the noise my little night
friends made that I had a hard time falling asleep if they didn't
come out for whatever reason.

I poured a bowl of water into the wok, scrubbed off the rust
with a vegetable sponge, then scooped out the brownish water.
The iron wok was fixed to the stove, its edge sealed with lime so
that smoke and heat wouldn't escape from the crack. Tonight I
was going to make myself and my pets some vegetable porridge
with the leftover rice in the basket. When I took the basket off
the hook and lifted the cloth, a slimy, sour smell got into my
nose. Shit! The rice had gone bad again—for the third time this
month. I must think of another way of handling my meals because the days were getting hotter and hotter. Last time, I ate
the bad rice and had diarrhea for a week. Since there was no
bathroom in the fields, I had to solve my urgent need in the tall
grass or behind the trees.

"All right then," I said loudly to Hong Hong and Yaya, who
had been circling around my feet since we came back, a sign
that they were hungry, "we'll make a nice fresh meal for tonight. Only it'll take some time, so I need your patience, okay?"

They nodded as if they understood me. I sat down on the low stool behind the stove and cleaned the ash out of the hole. I poured three bowls of water into the wok, then two bowls of rice, one chopped cabbage, five potatoes, two spoons of lard, and finally, salt. That would make a good vegetable rice meal. The lard would give it the flavor of pork, which I hadn't tasted for so long. Recently I'd been dreaming about the fat pork I hated as a kid. Mother used to order my sister and me to swallow the fatty chunks, saying it would help us grow. Sea Cloud sometimes was able to get out of it with her tears or charm. Since I didn't know how to cry or plead, I had no choice but to swallow every chunk of fat pork Mother put in my bowl. The gagging sensation caused by the slimy, greasy chunks sliding down my throat haunted my nights. I dreamed over and over again that I was eating worms and I had to say Thanks to the person who forced the crawling creatures into my mouth.

But now I really missed fat pork.

I inserted three dry pine twigs into the stove and spread some rice straw on top. They easily kindled into a nice fire. Steam soon puffed out, filling the room with a white mist, that mingled with the smoke from the fire. I tucked a towel around the wok to prevent too much steam from escaping. The cover Mother gave me didn't match the wok well. The rice often came out half-cooked. Soon the ashes that had accumulated in the stove began making heavy black smoke. I put another pine twig in the stove and stirred gently with a poker. The twig exploded into flames. Hissing juice started oozing out from the end of the twig, as if crying for its last moment of life. Sparks were flying around underneath the wok. They reminded me of the mornings in the Navy compound when I lit the small coal stove and fanned it while counting sparks and watching the orange flames absorb my white breath.

The soft cackles of Yaya and Hong Hong disturbed my reverie. I stroked their silky feathers. Their smoothness always calmed me down. Sometimes I felt I might have been a hen or a duck in my previous life.

Two bundles of straws were burnt. I stood up, cleaned the soot off the cover, and unwound the towel. It's got to come out good, it's got to, I chanted to myself. I lifted the cover, but couldn't see anything through the steam. I picked some rice with a spoon and tasted it. Shit! shit! shit! I screamed, throwing the cover and spoon against the wall. Thanks to the crooked cover, the rice had come out half-cooked again. This was too much. Hunger and exhaustion suddenly overwhelmed me. I sat on the mud floor. Tears flooded down my cheeks. A freshly cooked meal, that was all I asked for after a long day of work in the fields under the scorching sun. Was that too much? Half-cooked rice. How long would this life last? When would I be able to leave this dim, muddy room and sit in a college classroom?

Something rubbed against my ankles. I looked down and saw Yaya squatting between my bare feet, her flat beak knocking against my leg gently and persistently as if she were determined to pull me out of this hysterical mood. Hong Hong was looking up at me anxiously. She jumped on my knees as soon as our eyes met. I buried my face in her red feathers and rocked back and forth, humming an improvised song. As the pitch of my voice rose higher, Hong Hong began shaking her head vigorously as if she were drunk. I laughed.

I wiped my tears and decided to make another wok of vegetable rice. I stood up to check the water jar. It was empty. I yoked my barrels and walked to the well, which was a mile away to the east of the village. Yaya and Hong Hong followed behind. We strolled along the stream that divided Lishao Village into two parts. The crystal running water splashed against the gray pebbles at the bottom of the stream. I waded into it and soaked my hands in the cool water. A baby fish bumped into my leg and swam away in panic. It made me laugh for a long time. If Sea Cloud were here, she wouldn't let it escape. She was born to be a fisherwoman.

I looked back at Lishao. Smoke rose so slowly from the chimneys that it looked immobile, like columns connecting the sky and the earth. Yaya was swimming in the stream, diving occasionally for a fish. Hong Hong was chasing a grasshopper on the bank. Somewhere down the stream, peasant women were washing vegetables and clothes. Their wild laughter, instead of breaking the peace of the landscape, brought greater harmony to my soul. I scooped up a handful of water and drank it. It tasted sweet. I fetched my barrels from the bank and filled them with the cool stream water. It would make a better meal for tonight than the well water.

Twenty-five minutes later, I put an extraordinarily large bowl of vegetable rice on the table, shouting, "Hong Hong, Yaya, dinner is ready."

THE
STORY
OF
Ju

⌒ Ju hung herself on the eve of her wedding. When her half-witted stepbrother ran around the village shouting out the news, I was just picking up the note Ju had slipped under my door three days earlier. The dusty note, folded in the shape of a swallow, sent chills down my spine. It read:

Dear Teacher,

My father sold me to a blind man in a fishing village. It's an exchange marriage. I marry that guy, and his younger sister, who is as blind as her brother, will be engaged to my stepbrother, plus 200 yuan as a betrothal gift. Not bad, eh? I didn't know I was worth so much.

It's funny that Mom's third husband has one eye and my future husband has none. It seems that my fate is worse than my mother's. But I don't have to take it, do I?

On Lantern's Day, someone will come to fetch me and take me to Lao Village, where my husband lives.

There'll be no ceremony. Not necessary since I'm just
a commodity in a trade deal. But I'm not going to let
it happen. I'm not for sale.

I hope I can see you one last time before I'm gone.
Only three days left. Not much time. If not, I still have
the book you gave me. It's as good as seeing you.

Your student,

Ju

I rushed outside. Peasants were shouting in excitement as
they ran toward the hut where Ju lived with her family. When
I got there, a crowd had already gathered in the yard, whispering to one another and trying to squeeze into the room. Inside,
Ju's stepgrandmother and stepfather were cursing at Ju's
mother for having raised such scum. Two angry strangers were
standing at the door. I was wondering who they were when
they suddenly shouted that no one was to leave this house until
they got their 200 yuan of betrothal payment back. Some old
women smacked their lips and sighed heavily. They talked
about how Ah Liang, Ju's stepfather, couldn't return the betrothal gift since he had spent it all on the rice wine. And his
poor boy, with the kind of brain he had, would never be able to
get married. No one seemed to lament Ju's death except her
mother. Her sobbing sounded so weak and helpless in the commotion. I turned around at once and ran from the scene.

"She's only fourteen, she's only fourteen. And I could have
saved her. I could have saved her." I repeated this to myself as I
ran blindly along the stream. If I had returned to the village
from home a day earlier and found the note, Ju might still be
alive.

Fenli was waiting in my room. Her new pink cotton-padded
jacket reminded me that I was one of the bridesmaids at my best

friend Young Su's wedding. The ceremony would start in two hours and I was supposed to go over now to help her prepare. I started crying as I handed her Ju's letter, which had been crumbled in my fist. Fenli shook her head after reading it twice.

"No, you couldn't have saved her."

She was trying to comfort me, but I stared at her rosy cheeks with hostility. She and Ju belonged to different classes. Ju was an outcast. Her mother was regarded as a symbol of misfortune for having married three times. Her stepfather was a drunkard and her stepgrandma was a crazy woman with an evil tongue. Fenli, on the other hand, was the first daughter of the Party secretary of Lishao Village. She taught twenty-three village kids—grades one through six—in a one-room school. When she was a student, she had failed every subject except singing. If not for her father's influence, she wouldn't have been granted her elementary school diploma. She was one of the few privileged ones in the village. Shielded from the sun and rain, from the daily twelve-hour toil in the fields, she was the princess of the village. She had hardly ever spoken to Ju. So what right did she have to say that I couldn't have saved her?

Fenli folded the letter and inserted it into the *Communist Manifesto* on the desk.

"You shouldn't blame yourself too much," she said, rummaging through the pages with her fingers and sticking out her tongue as she saw the red lines I marked under some sentences. "What could you have done for her—help her run away? She knew it wouldn't work. She had seen her mother try to escape many times but end up crawling back home for shelter and food."

"I could have reported the situation to your father. He might have been able to do something, like persuade Ju's stepfather to stop the marriages or something. Your father has the power."

"No, you're wrong. He'd never have done that even if he had the kind of power you're talking about. In fact, the marriage could have been a perfect match, changing her life for the better. So what if the guy is blind and thirty-five years older than Ju? Nothing can be worse than the life she was leading in her stepfather's house. Besides, her would-be husband is a popular fortune-teller. That brings him good money and power. He has no relatives. Ju would have been the sole hostess in the house, no mother-in-law or sister-in-law to give her orders or troubles. What was best about the marriage was the location. The blind man lives in a fishing village. Do you know what that means? It means women there don't have to work in the fields. They sit at home with their friends, knitting fishing nets and chatting, and they have rice and seafood to eat every day instead of dried sweet potatoes and pickled cabbages. What a life she could have lived!"

I had to look away from Fenli for a second time to prevent myself from bloodying her nose. Not that she was talking nonsense. On the contrary, every word she uttered was absolutely true. Ju would have lived a life every peasant woman envies, except for the husband being blind and old. But why did I hate Fenli so much at that moment?

"If he's that great, maybe you can replace Ju and marry that fortune-teller. It will save your mother much trouble to go to Dinghai County every month to look for a husband for you," I said with a wry mouth.

The proud princess blushed deeply as if her cheeks were going to burst open. But she quickly jerked her head and looked straight into my eyes.

"We should all know our positions in this world and be content with them. Otherwise we'll end up in misery. All the peasants agreed that Ju should never have gone to school. The books had made her think too much. They blinded her eyes and turned her into a fool. You know what book she had tied around her waist when she hung herself? *Andersen's Fairy Tales!* What did she want—to be a mermaid? Everybody wanted to find out who gave her that book, but my father hushed it up."

For a moment I felt like all the blood was rushing from my head. I must have looked terribly pale because Fenli rushed forward to support me. I waved at her and told her to leave. I needed to rest for a few minutes before I went to Young Su's wedding. After she walked out of the door, I took out the note and stared at the neat handwriting. There were no grammatical or spelling mistakes in the letter. Ju had improved her writing a great deal within a year. I had taught her how to write and got her interested in books. I'd given Ju *Andersen's Fairy Tales,* hoping it would add a little color to her life. Was it really, as Fenli and the peasants believed, the cause of her death?

I had met Ju in a fifth-grade composition class at Ganlan People's Commune Elementary School. It was my first day subbing there, my first day standing in front of a classroom. I was still dazzled by this sudden, unexpected transaction. I had come to Lishao Village to be reeducated by the peasants; now I was going to be the teacher of their children.

That morning, I had just started cutting winter wheat when a boy called me from the end of the road and shouted out the message that Uncle Bao, the Party secretary of Lishao Production Brigade, wanted me immediately. I ran all the way to his house, which he used as his office. When I got there, he was digging a pit in the yard to store garbage and manure. When they fermented, they would produce methane which could be used as fuel.

"Uncle Bao, you sent for me?" I called into the pit, which was almost ten feet deep, keeping as far as possible from the edge so that he wouldn't appear to be below me. Men believed that if they went under women's lower bodies, it would bring them bad luck for at least a whole year.

"Yeah." He spat and ground his spit into the dirt with his bare foot. Then he squatted, took out a small pouch, poured some tobacco onto a piece of newspaper, and rolled a cigarette. He closed his eyes as he inhaled the smoke into his lungs and let it out slowly. He seemed to have forgotten about me.

"Congratulations!" he said at last, without looking up.

I jumped. I didn't remember having done anything worth being congratulated for. Was he just being sarcastic about something I had done wrong? I searched my brain, going over all my recent activities. Nothing seemed to have exceeded the bounds. I didn't drink or gamble, I worked every day.

"Uncle Bao is kidding," I said, forcing myself to smile down into the pit.

"You'll be a teacher."

I jumped again. Was he out of his mind?

"It's an honor in our village," Uncle Bao continued in his slow, authoritative way. "Among the 150 educated youths in Ganlan People's Commune, you were chosen to substitute for the teacher who's going to have a baby. Two months." He suddenly opened his eyes. "Go to school now. They're waiting for you. Be a good girl. I hope you won't disappoint me and our village."

I walked down the country road in a daze, not knowing whether I should be happy or worried. To be chosen as a teacher not only meant that I had won the trust of the Party but also that I would be spared the hard fieldwork for a while. The thought of facing a class of fifty students, however, made me tremble. I had not the slightest idea what to say to them or how to make them behave. To tell the truth, I was terrified of kids.

Fifth graders. I heard peasants started sending their children to school pretty late. Some fifth graders were already twelve or thirteen years old. There were only two or three years difference between us. Could I discipline them?

The school was about a half hour's walk from the village. I arrived during the ten-minute break. Students, mostly boys, were running around, crashing into one another with wild laughter. The assistant principal received me in her office, which she shared with eleven other teachers. The only sign to mark her position was her desk, twice as big as the teachers' desks and with four drawers. She handed me a copy of *The Beijing Review* in English.

"Read this article." She pointed to the first page.

Sweat started to pour from my face even before I had finished the first paragraph. Among the political jargon, the only words I recognized were "our great leader Chairman Mao," and "it," and "good." The assistant principal laughed derisively. She stopped me in the middle of a sentence and handed me an old Chinese textbook.

"Try the Chinese class first. You should have no problem with that, I suppose." She looked mockingly at me, then added, "Start with Lesson Three."

The bell rang. The yard echoed with threatening noises and running steps, then a dead silence.

"Your room is 5-2." She turned her back to me.

I dragged myself to the classroom. The textbook was smeared with black grease and chalk powder. Lesson Three. I had no idea what it was about. The damned woman could have let me take a look at the text instead of testing my English. Either she wanted to give me a head-on blow at the first encounter or she just didn't like me. Maybe both. But what was I going to say to the students, and how? I opened the door with a sinking heart.

"Stand up," a boy shouted. The class stood there, tall and

short, mostly in dark, shabby clothing, staring at me with wide eyes. I had never experienced a salute like this. It embarrassed and disarmed me. I froze at the door, not knowing what to do, for nearly five minutes, until someone started tittering. I suddenly realized that the class was waiting for my order to let them sit down.

"Please be seated," I said. My voice sounded strange, as if someone else were speaking through my body. "And take out your books."

I wrote *Lesson 3* on the blackboard. The class stared at me in silence. No one moved.

"I said take out your textbooks," I raised my voice, thinking they had already started testing me.

"We don't have no books," one of the boys in the front row shouted.

What? A class without textbooks? The assistant principal must be playing a joke on me. I stood in front of the class, furious, panicked. I had imagined every possible situation except this. I felt I was sinking to the bottom of a well and someone had put a cover over it.

"Why don't you have books?" I finally asked in despair.

Everyone tried to answer at the same time. Sold out. Short of paper. All used to print Mao's red books.

"What did your teacher do?" I asked, waving down the voices.

"She wrote the lesson on the board and we copied it." The boy who had answered my first question replied again. I noticed that he wasn't really shouting. He just had a very loud voice.

I felt sick as I copied the lesson on the board. It was as absurd as when my mother had forced me to copy hundreds of Mao's quotations and articles from magazines. I had cried, begged, and cursed, but my mother was very firm about this practice. These kids, however, didn't seem to mind it at all. The boy with a loud voice had a cold. Once in a while he would sniff the mucus back into his nose. I tried not to look in his direction.

The door opened a little. A girl in rags stood outside, staring at me as if I were an alien. Her gray face was streaked with sweat; she must have run all the way to school. I immediately excused her lateness.

"Are you a student in this class?" I asked quietly, trying not to disturb the class. She stood at the door, her bare feet and chapped lips slightly apart, her gaze void of any emotion or sign that she had heard me.

"What's your name?" I walked toward her. "Why don't you come in?"

She didn't move. Her blank, fixed stare reminded me of someone I knew.

"What's your name?" I asked again. My curiosity made me patient.

"Ju," the boy with a loud voice shouted from the back of the room, "Crazy Ju."

The class laughed. The boy stuck out his tongue and withdrew his head into his neck like a turtle.

Ju's gaze turned in his direction. "Fuck your mother." Her thick lips hardly moved as she uttered the curse.

"Ju, come in and sit down." I pretended not to hear the curse. For some reason, I didn't want to discipline her at all.

She walked heavily to the last row. I suddenly realized who she reminded me of—Hua, Crazy Hua. She had married Ah Liang in the first month after I settled in Lishao Village. That was her third marriage. The deaths of her first and second husbands had made her a symbol of bad luck—star of white tiger—a man killer. When Hua lost her second husband, her mother-in-law was anxious to get rid of her so she could take back the house. The matchmaker persuaded Ah Liang and his mother that their stars in the cosmos were in a much more powerful position than Hua's. The death of Ah Liang's first wife was proof of this. They were both in the tractor when the accident took place. She was killed, together with five other people. He was the only survivor, although he lost an eye and half his stomach. Nobody could harm Ah Liang any more after that. So Ah Liang chose a lucky day and went to Waishao, Lishao's sister village, to bring Hua and her daughter home. There was no ceremony. A woman who has been married three times was an embarrassment to herself and her family. In the rain, Hua and her daughter climbed over the Lu Mountain carrying a basket of steamed bread as a dowry, and followed Ah Liang to his hut outside the village. When they passed by the rice paddy, the peasants stopped weeding and shouted some dirty jokes to them. I didn't get a chance to take a good look because they covered their heads with huge bamboo hats. They looked more like mourners going to a funeral than newlyweds going to a bridal chamber, a new home.

The next day, Hua joined us in the fields with a swollen, bruised face. Someone who had eavesdropped outside Ah Liang's window said that Hua wouldn't sleep with him because Ah Liang wanted her thirteen-year-old daughter to start working in the fields the next day. Hua had agreed to marry him on the condition that her daughter be allowed to finish elementary school in the commune. Their fight incensed his mother. She shouted to her son to kick the ass of the white tigress. The peasants all laughed. This woman was really crazy. Could her daughter make a living on that diploma? Could that piece of paper help her find a rich husband? They teased her and questioned her about her first night with Ah Liang. Hua kept her mouth shut. Her swollen eyes were half open, half closed, as if the outside world didn't exist. After that, she came to work every day, often starved and badly bruised. Ah Liang's mother locked up all the food. Hua's daughter couldn't get any because she wasn't working. So whatever Hua was given, she shared with her daughter.

I walked to the newcomer's seat and sat down next to her. She didn't really look like Hua, but her eyes had the same kind of despair and indifference.

"Are you from Lishao?" I asked.

She nodded. So she was Hua's daughter. With one glance, I could see her wretched life in the house of the ferocious old woman and the alcoholic stepfather. Her patched clothing, her uncombed hair, her smell, her hands and cheeks scarred from frostbite told everything. She actually passed my door every evening carrying a huge bundle of wood on her back, walking slowly toward Ah Liang's hut. But this was the first time I saw her this close.

"We're copying Lesson Three. Take your time. I'll wait for you."

Ju put her schoolbag on the desk. It was made of small patches of cloth in different colors and shapes. Her notebook was sewed together in the same way. Her pencil was so short that she could hardly hold it. However, she handled everything with care and dignity, ignoring my gaze and interest.

I paced around the classroom to pass the time as the students copied the lesson. The high windows were protected by thick wooden fences. Black eaves slanted over the walls, keeping the sun away from the room. The school was converted from an abandoned Buddhist convent. I leaned on the door and watched an old woman lighting a coal stove in the middle of the yard. A red rooster, his feathers and wings opened wide, was spinning around a white hen. The hen ignored his performance. She was only interested in the grasshopper the rooster had brought her. Suddenly he jumped on top of her.

"Jump." I smiled as I murmured this word to myself, remembering my ignorance in my childhood. When my father had asked my mother if our white rooster was able to jump, I cut in, "Yes, he can even jump onto the roof of the chicken coop." They laughed. Father pointed his finger at me while wiping his eyes, "Oh, how stupid, how stupid this child is!" I responded through my tears, "I saw it jump with my own eyes."

The mating lasted only a second. The hen shook her feathers indifferently. Jump. It was in Lishao Village that I learned what it meant. One day, Young Guo, the brother of my new girl friend Young Su, said he had something interesting to show me. He took me to Uncle Bao's backyard where a crowd had gathered around a sow howling in the mud. A stranger led in a hog. His tiny tail hung comically over his enormous balls. The sow stopped screaming when she saw the hog. As soon as the hog jumped on top of her, the male peasants began cheering. The women giggled, covering their mouths or their eyes with their aprons. Young Guo nudged me with his elbow, "Seaweed, can you howl? I bet you can't. I bet you've never howled."

"Of course I can. It's the easiest thing in the world." I shouted, then immediately realized the trap I had fallen in. Too late. The peasants roared with laughter.

"Finished," a student shouted as she leaned on the desk behind her and heaved a sigh.

"What did your teacher do after this?" I asked.

"Read, summarize, and write an essay," a boy answered. He was the only one in the room who was decently dressed.

"No writing, son of a bitch, no writing!" some students yelled at him. They had discovered my lack of experience and tried to take advantage to avoid work.

"Yes, there is. I can prove it," the well-dressed boy shouted back, shaking his notebook. The class was a mess. The boys argued with one another whether they should do the writing next. And the girls giggled like hens that had just laid eggs. The noise made me dizzy.

"Quiet!" I shouted, beating my desk with a bamboo stick I had found behind the door. They all turned toward me and closed their mouths. "We shall do writing today," I said firmly. Their compliance to my violent reaction gave me some confidence. "And the topic is . . . " I paused. I wasn't prepared for this. I had no idea what they should write about. "Well, write anything you want."

"We've never done this. Our teacher always gave us a topic," the well-dressed boy said timidly.

"Well, I'm your teacher now. Do what I tell you and write whatever you feel like. It's the easiest thing in the world."

They moaned as they took out their writing paper, utterly confused by this freedom. Soon the room was noisy again. Some talked loudly and some threw wads of paper at each other. I noticed Ju was carving something on her desk. I walked over and saw a skeleton and two bones crossing each other. The knife, with its delicate carvings on the bronze handle, looked out of place in Ju's dirty hand.

"What are you doing, Ju?"

She leapt from her bench, hiding the knife behind her back.

"Did you finish your writing?"

No answer. I looked at the skeleton. Perfect. She must have practiced it many times.

"Give me the knife," I said. I was curious about it. Where did she get that expensive knife?

"No," she said loudly. Apparently she thought I was going to confiscate it. The room suddenly became quiet. Everyone was watching us. I grabbed her arm. Ju clutched at her knife as if she was fighting for her life. I pulled harder. In the struggle, I sliced my hand on the blade. A girl screamed as she saw the blood.

"Principal, principal," she yelled as she began to run out. I freed Ju and caught the girl at the door. I didn't want to see the assistant principal's face at this moment.

"Go back to your seats and finish your work, right now," I ordered. The bleeding gave me more authority. Everyone started writing except for Ju. No one complained or moaned. I wrapped my finger with a handkerchief, wondering how I should handle this incident. I wasn't mad at Ju at all. In fact, it was silly of me to grab her knife like that. But of course, I couldn't admit it to the class. And I had to do something with Ju to show the class that I was their teacher. Ju sat motionless at her desk, the knife clutched in her hand. Her face, still expressionless, made me extremely sad. I wished I could tell her that everything was okay, that I wasn't going to punish her.

The bell rang. The students handed me their writing, eyeing me curiously to see how I was going to punish Ju. I waited till they had all left the classroom and then closed the door. When I sat down next to Ju, her body stiffened and she cringed as though she was about to be hit in the stomach. I felt the pain for her. I knew exactly what it was like to anticipate punishment: you were torn between the wish to get it over with as soon as possible and the wish to put it off as long as possible.

"It's all right, Ju," I said with my gentlest tone. "Just tell me who gave you this knife. It's a real beauty."

She looked up, her eyes flashed a moment of hope, then clouded immediately with disbelief. "My mom gave it to me," she answered with reluctance. "She got it from her dad, my *waigong*. My mom said he was a scholar, a graduate from the high school in the county, and she wants me to be a scholar too, just like my grandpa. People will treat us nice and respect us."

My heart sank. How could I tell her that a high school diploma no longer meant anything, that scholars nowadays were nothing but *chou lao jiu*—stinky No. 9—the lowest class among the landlords, counter-revolutionists, hoodlums, rightists, and other class enemies of our society. My high school education got me nowhere but to this village to be reeducated by the peasants.

"Why don't you go home, Ju?" I sighed. "I'll see you tomorrow. Try not to be late again."

She looked into my eyes to see if I meant it. I nodded my head. She stood up and packed her bag slowly as if she was giving me time to change my mind. When she finished packing, she turned to me and asked, her hands opens,

"I can go, just like this?"

"Just like this," I answered, trying to smile.

She stood before me, her back slightly bent forward, probably developed from carrying heavy loads every day. The frozen look on her face had become her permanent mask, but tears were gathering in her eyes. She blinked and swallowed, but two drops still fell. Before I could think of some comforting words, she ran out.

I sat up that night reading the papers. Though I let them choose their own topics, they all wrote about the article they'd copied from the blackboard, using the same political slogans found in newspapers and magazines. The next morning I stood in front of the class, and stared at them for five minutes without a word.

"Do you like writing?" I finally asked.

No one answered.

"I hated it when I was at school. And you?"

Yes, they all laughed and shouted.

"Why do you hate it?"

They looked at one another, still afraid and puzzled.

"I'll read your papers, and you'll understand why."

All the essays sounded as if they were written by the same person. When I started the third paper, the class laughed hysterically. Even Ju looked up and smiled through her mask. I shook the paper in my hand and asked, "Do you know what you wrote about? Who is Confucius? Why do you want to throw him on the ground and stamp your feet on him? What is Marxism, capitalism and revisionism? Who can explain what you've written?"

Finally the boy with a loud voice answered, "We've been taught to write this way ever since we started school."

"How about trying something you're familiar with. For example, you all have to come to school every morning. Talk about it, then. Tell me when you get up, what you do, how you come here, and what you see on your way. Write simply and clearly. Forget about the words you copied from the textbooks and newspapers. Start right now."

They took out their notebooks, confused but excited. Everyone was thinking hard, yet after ten minutes, no one was able to put down a word. Someone shouted, "Teacher, I don't know how to do it. I just can't write anything."

"Just tell me what you did since you got up this morning and what you saw. Be specific."

As I walked around the classroom, I heard the teacher in the next classroom disciplining her students in a whining tone, and I wondered if I sounded the same yesterday. Ju put down her pencil and looked up. She had pretty dark eyes, I noticed.

"Finished?"

She nodded and handed me the self-made notebook. Her handwriting was neat and small. To save paper, I thought, as I read it eagerly:

My house has no clock. The red cock tells me the
time. I get up when it crows. I put on my clothing. I

cook breakfast for the family. I cut a basket of grass in the fields for the pigs. I sweep the hall and yard. This morning I ate a half bowl of dried sweet potato porridge. I washed the bowls. I took my school bag. I didn't have a watch. How long I walked, I didn't know. There was fog on the mountains. Today would be a good day, I thought. I hurried to school. I sat down, had class. I wasn't late today.

I looked up and saw the whole class was watching me intensely. I smiled at Ju and said, "Good." All the other students smiled too, as if I were praising them. They resumed their writing in excitement. When the monitor collected the papers, I picked out Ju's notebook and started reading.

They laughed, with surprise and admiration.

"Don't laugh. True, she made some mistakes. But she told us a lot of things, and she noticed that the fog would bring a good day. It's much better than the boring stuff you gave me yesterday. I want you to keep writing like this."

For the following class, I asked them to write about their families, where they lived, what they did at home, and how they felt about school. Again Ju finished her paper ahead of the others. She tore the page with her writing from her notebook, folded it into a swallow-shaped note, and waited at her desk for the bell. When her classmates left the room for lunch, she came over to me and slipped the note into my hand. "Please read it after class," she said and ran out.

I read it as soon as I got home:

> Going to school is my happiest moment. At school, there's no stepgrandma screaming and cursing. She's a tigress. No stepfather drinking and threatening to beat up my mom and me. And no mom crying. I like

school. I can do anything for school. Every morning I
get up early to do my duties—cooking, cutting grass,
cleaning the house. I don't mind the chores, because I
can go to school afterwards. I like school. Some classmates laugh me. My clothing is dirty, my hair smells.
I'm poor. I pick everything I need from garbage. I
don't mind. I like school. I want to stay in school forever. But I also want to graduate soon, so that I can
work. I'm thirteen now, time for me to help mom.
When I have money, the first thing I'll do is to buy a
big meal for my mom and myself, the second is to get
us out of that wretched house. I like school. Here I
have books to read. I can sit quiet and dream. Now I
have a nice teacher.

I wished I could hold Ju in my arms, comb her hair, talk to
her, and make her laugh, things that an older sister would do
to a crying younger sister. This was something new for me. I
had two sisters. I grew up with Sea Cloud—we shared the same
bed, went to the same school—but I had never thought of
touching her or holding her hand. All I felt about her was jealousy and anger. For a while, I felt protective toward my brother,
Sea Tiger. But when he grew up, he gradually preferred the
company of Sea Cloud, who was much more outgoing and ex-
citing. One thing was certain: neither of them needed my protection or help.

For five days Ju hadn't shown up for class. After school, I
went to the fields where the villagers worked, hoping to talk to
her mother or stepfather. To my surprise, only Ah Liang was
around. In my memory, Hua had never missed a day to earn the
3.5 working points, the major income source for the family. Ah
Liang made 8.5 working points a day, but he was drunk most of

the time passed out on the kitchen floor. I rolled up my pants and waded into the rice paddy. The peasants greeted me with whistles and friendly curses. They were surprised as well as flattered that I went back to work with them in the fields.

"Hey, you, what are you doing here, teacher? You're not fired, I hope?" Young Guo shouted at me.

"Get lost," I said and found a place next to Aunt Wang. She knew all the gossip in and outside the village.

"Hey, Aunt Wang, where's Hua?"

"Ha, this isn't news anymore. She ran away." Before I could tell her to lower her voice, she had turned to Ah Liang. "Brother Liang, how many times has she done it, five or six?"

I should have known better. Aunt Wang had the reputation of being a "loud speaker." Her husband used to beat her up every day to stop her from gossiping and making trouble. But it was useless. Gossiping was part of her life. She had been married for ten years but never gotten pregnant once. The doctors said her husband's sperm were too weak, but no one believed it. If a woman couldn't have babies, whose fault could it be but her own?

Ah Liang pulled at the weeds sullenly. He didn't bother looking up to answer Aunt Wang's question.

"Be careful, Aunt Wang," a young peasant warned her with a sly smile. "Ah Liang hasn't had a bed partner for five nights in a row. He has accumulated lots of fire in his balls. Don't let him explode on you."

"Fuck you." Ah Liang spat and threw a handful of mud at him. Everyone laughed.

I was anxious to know what had happened to Ju. What did her mother's escape have to do with her absence from school? Did she run away with her mother? I looked around, hoping someone would mention Ju's name. But no one seemed to want to talk about her. Aunt Wang had already been pulled away from me by her husband. And Ah Liang's bloody stare was too frightening. I worked silently until it was time to go home.

Another three days passed. The villagers, involved with their own busy lives, seemed to have forgotten about Hua's escape. At dusk, I stood on the road where Ju used to pass with a bundle of firewood on her back. Someone did show up carrying firewood, but it was her stepbrother, the son of Ah Liang's first marriage. When I tried to talk to him, he mumbled something and walked away as fast as he could.

Ten days later, Ju appeared in my class. She looked pale and tired. There was a wound on her face. It cut through her right eyebrow and ended on her right cheekbone. Still red and swollen, it looked like a leech with a stomach full of blood. For the whole morning, she sat like a statue, staring into space. Her dark empty eyes recognized no one. When the bell rang, she didn't move. I waited patiently at my desk, afraid that if I talked, she might run away. Finally she walked up to me and handed me a roll of paper. "My homework for the past ten days," she said in a whisper and left abruptly.

I read it on the way home.

> Mom ran away. I helped her. Two days they didn't give her nothing to eat, just because she broke a bowl. They beat her so hard that they broke two broom handles. They made her kneel on the broken pieces of the bowl. When she fainted, they tied her to a ridge pole. I hate them, with my whole heart and guts. At night I cut the rope and released her. We cried silently. Mom said she was hungry. There was no food around in the house. So she decided to go to other villages, maybe even to Dinghai County. It's much easier to

find food in the city. There are garbage cans and restaurant leftovers. Maybe she can even find a job as a
maid or nanny. When she settles down there, she'll
send for me and we can live together, just by ourselves, no man. Maybe I can even go to middle school
after I graduate from the sixth grade. Mom smiled as
she kept talking. I smiled too, not because I believed in
her dreams, but because it makes me happy to see her
happy. How can she even get to the city without any
money to buy a bus ticket?

They were so mad that Mom escaped. They locked
me up at night and made me do all the housework
during the day. I was hungry. For two days I didn't eat
anything. The old tigress cursed and spat at me all day
long. I don't mind. Working and starving, no problem. But I miss school. I miss my teacher and classmates. I couldn't stop crying at night.

I was scared. Stepfather was drunk tonight as he
staggered into my room with a full bowl of rice wine.
He looked at me with his bloodshot eyes and mumbled, "Your mom ran away. You must replace her."
He bent over the chair to which I was tied and sniffed
at my hair like a dog. I kicked at his shin as hard as I
could. He screamed in pain and hit my forehead with
the bowl. I fainted. I woke up with sharp pains all over
my face. Someone was biting my cheeks really hard. I
opened my eyes and saw my stepfather's bloody face.
I screamed and pushed him to the floor. He was too
drunk to get up. Soon he started snoring in his sleep.
I ran into the pig sty and cried and cried. For the first
time I wish Mom hadn't gone.

Mom came back the next morning. She crawled
back, too hungry to walk. Nobody in the neighboring

villages dared to give her food. They were all afraid of the tigress' curses. She couldn't go to Dinghai either. No one would give her a lift. She said she was worried about me so she came back. Surprising that that didn't beat her. They even gave her a bowl of sweet potatoes. But she had to go to work immediately.

I'm happy I can go to school again. I'm also sad because I want mom to leave this house forever. With me. To some nice place. A lot of food. A lot of friends. We'd live happily together.

I cried angrily. I was furious with Ah Liang, his mother, and the villagers who pretended not to see what was happening to Hua and Ju. The misery of others provided them with materials for gossip. I was also furious with myself. I could do nothing to help them.

The spring ploughing season came. Unlike other schools, Ganlan Elementary didn't give the students a one-week vacation to help out their families. Instead, they organized the students to go to different villages to work in the fields. This way, all the teachers would have to participate in the work instead of hanging around in idleness. The grade I taught was assigned to cut and dry grass to feed the village water buffalos in winter. When I announced the news, the students asked, "What's the topic for our composition?"

"I appreciate your enthusiasm, but don't you think it's too early to think about it now? We haven't started the work yet, for God's sake."

"Come on, give us the topic so that we can be done with the writing and enjoy our vacation," a boy begged. "Our ex-teacher always let us do this."

"But how can you write about things before they take place?"

I was quite unhappy. I thought they'd really begun to like writing, and they had asked for the topic because they were enthusiastic about it.

"You don't believe? We can bet!"

I looked in the direction of the voice. It was Ju. All the other students also turned to her in surprise. Ju had never spoken out in class.

If it had been someone else, I would have ignored them. What was on Ju's mind today? She was even smiling mysteriously.

"All right, Ju. What do you want to bet on?"

"The book." Her eyes sparkled.

The class stirred with excitement. I took a deep breath. Ju wanted *Andersen's Fairy Tales*, my most precious book. After my first copy was confiscated, I searched for a whole year for another copy and traded five of my best novels to get it. I had torn off the front and back covers and glued on the red plastic cover of Mao's book to disguise the content. For the past two weeks, I had been reading the stories to the class before I dismissed them. I trusted them. They wouldn't report to the principal that I read a poisonous Western book to them. Ju always listened with her head tilted toward her left shoulder, her expression still blank but no longer cold and desperate.

"All right," I said. If the book could make her happy, I was willing to part with it. "But I don't think you can win. First of all, you don't even know what the weather will be like tomorrow, where we're going to cut grass, and how many people will go."

Ju smiled mysteriously. "I can solve those problems. Only I have a request. Can we cut the grass near Lishao Village? I know some good spots."

We agreed and decided to meet at the gate of Lishao Village at six o'clock the next morning. That night, I wrapped *Andersen's*

Fairy Tales in red paper, along with a red velvet notebook and a fountain pen. Whether Ju won or lost, I wanted her to have the book. It made my happy to think how pleased she would be to hold the book in her hands. It wouldn't change her life, but at least it could take her away from her present misery for a few hours.

When we arrived at the village gate, Ju was already there, wiping her sweat with a towel. She was leaning on a pile of green grass tied in bundles that almost reached her head. She stepped toward us, holding a piece of paper in one hand, pointing with the other at my bag containing the package I had wrapped last night.

"Here's my essay about today's work. I have won." Her voice was confident, though she was trembling with the excitement of winning the book. "My mom and I got up at one o'clock and worked till five. Then I wrote the paper."

A woman appeared from the thick cover of the morning fog. She unloaded a big bundle of grass off her back. "Is this enough, darling?"

It was Ju's mother, Crazy Hua. We all stared at her in amazement. She was wearing the same rags she wore every day, patches upon patches, her hair still tangled and dusty, yet today she looked transformed. Something in her voice and her eyes when she looked at her daughter held everyone in awe.

"Yes, Mom. Take a rest. We'll go home when we get the book." Ju looked at her mother proudly.

Hua took off her apron and wiped the sweat from her daughter's face. I suddenly realized what caused Hua to look so different. It was her love for Ju. She would sacrifice her life for her daughter's happiness. For a moment, I felt jealous. If only my mother could love me like this!

I took out the parcel. "Here's the book, Ju. But I can't say you won, because our bet was whether someone could do a piece of good writing on an event before it takes place. You just told me you wrote your composition after you cut the grass. You still need to experience things to write about them. But I want to give you the book because you're sincere and hardworking."

The class applauded. Ju looked at the parcel in her hands and pressed it to her heart. She bit her lips so hard that she left a line of teethmarks beneath her lower lip. Suddenly she handed it back to me. "I lost. I'm not going to take it."

I thought for a moment, then opened the parcel and took out the notebook. "Take the notebook, then. If you want, you can copy the stories from the book in my class."

For the next two weeks, Ju worked hard on *Andersen's Fairy Tales*. The first story she did was "The Little Mermaid." It took her more than a week to finish it because she refused to give up her writing time to copy the story and she had to go home after school. The only time she had was during lunch break and the ten-minute recesses between classes. Before she could finish the next story, I was notified that the teacher I had been subbing for was coming back in two days. The last assignment I gave the class was to write about their mothers, but I said nothing about my leaving. What if someone started crying or no one showed *any* concern? I couldn't stand either possibility. Everyone worked hard, as if they secretly knew this would be their last chance to write about their feelings. When the bell rang, they all handed me their papers and ran out. Even Ju didn't stay to copy the story. Her writing filled three pages. For the first time, she didn't write on both sides to save paper. It read:

My mother is the best and kindest woman in the world.

She works very hard. Day and night. In summer she sits up late, fanning mosquitoes away for me. We can't afford mosquito nets or incense. Mom has very little food to eat every day. Stepgrandmother and stepfather said she only makes three and a half working points a day, less than a fourteen-year-old boy can earn. That's what she deserves to have. But Mother still saves her food for me, because I get nothing since I'm not working in the fields. They said the housework I do pays for my lodging. Mom wants me to grow well so I can read and write books. I read "The Little Mermaid" to her. She likes it very much. She is very proud of me. Nobody will dare take advantage of me when I have knowledge, and I'll have a better future than her, she said. I don't quite believe it but I don't want to hurt her. She married my stepfather because he agreed to take me in and let me continue my schooling. People think my mom is crazy. They make fun of her. But I think she's the best mother. I know it. I must study hard and grow fast so that I can speak for her someday.

Last night my stepfather beat Mom again and didn't give her food. She got up slowly this morning. Her eyes black and blue. She looked ill and needed rest. But stepfather said she must work to earn her food. Mom watched me eat breakfast. Study hard, she said, then walked out slowly. I watched her back. The sun came out white this morning. She had climbed on the top of the hill and was walking into the white sun. I wish I could follow her and enter the sun with her, and never come back.

I walked to the door and looked up at the sky until the sun blinded my eyes. Then I walked back to my desk and wrote on the first page of *Andersen's Fairy Tales*: "To Ju, my best friend." I was going to sign my name, then had a second thought. Ju would know where the book came from. But if someone else found out that I'd given it to her, I'd be in big trouble. So I wrapped it with an old newspaper and put it in Ju's schoolbag.

I never saw Ju again. I couldn't visit her house, which was guarded by a ferocious dog. She never passed my door again on her way to collect firewood. However, she slipped several notes under my door, with writings about her life in school and at home. Her teacher resumed the old method of writing. Everyone hated it, but no one dared complain. Her mother ran away again and was sent back by the neighborhood villagers when she fainted on the country road. In her last note, she told me that she probably wouldn't be able to finish the sixth grade. Her stepfather beat up her mother every day and blamed their poverty on her daughter. Ju had begged her mother to let her work in the fields, but she refused, saying she'd rather die than give up their last hope. When I got the note, I went to school to look for Ju. Too late. The teacher told me coldly that Ju had quit school and was going to get married to a rich man. When I left the room, she added that the less I messed up Ju's mind, the better off she would be. I was taken aback. Had she discovered the book I gave Ju? I was anxious for Ju but had no way to contact her. I only hoped what the teacher had told me was true: that Ju was going to marry a rich man. It was with this vague hope that I had left Lishao Village to spend my New Year's vacation at home in Dinghai County. When I returned, I was so busy distributing presents to Uncle Bao and his family members and other villagers that I didn't notice the death note Ju had put under my door.

Firecrackers exploded outside my room. Someone shouted, "Quick, bring more benches, rocks, and pine wood. They're only a few miles away." I recognized Young Guo's voice. He and his buddies were building a toll gate for the Sha villagers who were on their way here to fetch Young Su's dower. It was a local custom that the bride's family, usually represented by her brother, demanded a toll fee. The more money he could extract, the worthier the bride would look in the eyes of both families. Laughter broke out constantly as the group worked on the construction. Young Guo instructed his young friends to add a rock here, a pile of wood there, his voice intoxicated with joy, excitement, and authority. Who could believe that only half an hour before, he had stood on his tip toes in the crowd outside Ju's house, trying to catch a glimpse of the corpse of a fourteen-year-old girl who was supposed to get married on the same day as his sister? Now he seemed to have completely erased Ju's death and her mother's desperate sobs from his memory.

"It's not fair, it's not fair!" I pounded my desk with my fists, shouting at the top of my voice. The cup was knocked over, and a stream of tea flowed quickly to a book lying on the corner of my desk. I picked it up and realized it was the gift I had brought home for Ju, a book of fairy tales by the Grimm Brothers. I had worried about how I was going to give it to her, but now she no longer needed it. Had she needed it in the beginning? If she hadn't learned how to read and write, or hadn't read the book I had given her, would she still be alive?

I had always believed that knowledge was power and the only place to gain it was in college. Since universities admitted students only from the army, factories, and countryside at that time, I decided to move my city residence registration card to Lishao Village to become a peasant so that I could be recommended to college after two years of work. It was a real gamble: the odds of educated youths like me going on to college were a thousand to one. That meant I might be stuck on the farm for the rest of my life. But it was the only route, and I was willing to run the risk. Ju's mother also believed that knowledge could change her daughter's life. She had married Ah Liang so that Ju could graduate with a diploma. She and Ju had almost starved to death in order to be able to read and write. But what good had it brought them? My heart and soul suddenly filled with fear. What if my belief was also an illusion? What if I would never get out of this village?

Someone stroked my hair. I looked up and saw Fenli's grandma. Fenli was standing behind her holding a pink cotton-padded jacket. It was my bridesmaid uniform. I put my arms around Grandma Bao and buried my face in her soft belly. She patted my back gently without a word. Finally she pulled me up and wiped my wet cheeks with her apron.

"Now child, listen to me. The dead are dead, and we must go on. It's nobody's fault. Everything is fated. And we must accept it without complaint. Put on the jacket now and go to Young Su's wedding."

I lived in Lishao Village for sixteen more months. Ganlan Elementary asked me several times to sub, but I declined. It seemed much simpler and more rewarding to work in the fields. At the end of my third year in Lishao, I was finally recommended to Hangzhou Foreign Language School to study English and be trained to teach in a middle school. I had applied to the English Department of Hangzhou University. They gave me the highest mark on the oral exam, which was the only test for language ability, but the department accepted another girl whose uncle was a friend of the university president. I could do nothing about it. If I didn't go to Hangzhou Foreign Language School, even though it wasn't my first choice, I would probably have to wait another three years. I'd be too old then. I was eighteen but already felt like a twenty-eight-year-old spinster. The farm work and vegetarian diet had exhausted me. I was anxious to return to the city and live a normal life, a life with weekends, holidays, entertainments, and decent food. Although Hangzhou Foreign Language School wasn't a college, it was a professional school and I'd be guaranteed a teaching job after I graduated. It was practical. Besides, it was next to the Hangzhou University campus. So it was almost as good as a college. After three years in Lishao Village, I'd learned how to compromise. Or using Fenli's words, I'd learned to know where my position was located in society. Fenli herself had just married an accountant in the commune's grocery store. He was the son of the Waishao Village Party secretary. She had given up searching for a husband in the city after Ju's suicide. Now she was three month's pregnant and very happy.

On the day of my departure, I went to visit Ju's grave on top of Lu Mountain. Next to her mound was her mother's tomb. She had died two weeks after her daughter's death. The tombs had no stones, lying obscurely among the knee-high grasses like two abandoned straw hats. I picked some wild chrysanthemums for Ju and Hua. White liquid oozed from the broken stems like drops of milky tears. Sitting in front of the graves, I sobbed for Ju, whose life ended even before it began, and for Hua, whose life was nothing but misery and waste, and for myself, who had grown old—very, very old—at the age of eighteen, in order to live.

SUBWAY
RHAPSODY

Saturday night. Times Square. I had been groping in the subway maze for an hour. The entrance to the steps that led down to the 7 train platform was blocked with a chain and a piece of cardboard dangling from it: TAKE BMT TO QUEENS PLAZA FOR THE 7 TRAIN. What was BMT? I had seen the sign everywhere in this underground world and heard it everyday on the deafening subway loudspeakers, but I had never seen one single train marked BMT. Fortunately, there was an arrow on the cardboard indicating the direction. After I walked through several zigzagging hallways, took one escalator up and two flights down, I finally came to a small plaza. A bookstall caught my eye. Three rows of books lying neatly on the board. In the middle a book stood on a small easel like a rising sun. To my surprise, all these books had the same fiery orange color, the same words in bold gold letters against a silver background in the shape of a bomb explosion: THE BEST SELLER. It must be an extremely important book if it could take over the whole stand like Mao's little precious book, which occupied every bookstore in China during the Cultural Revolution. I squinted my eyes to see the title and the author, but the busy design and burning colors blurred everything on the cover into a fireball. I walked toward the stand, wondering where the owner was, when a woman in a blue coat leapt out from behind a column and blocked my way. She was skinny and tall, as if she had been walking around on stilts for so long that the wooden sticks had become part of her body. She bent toward me, her bony nose almost touching my forehead.

"English, eh, English?" she asked, waving the orange book fanatically under my nose.

I nodded, half scared, half fascinated by the feverish look in her eyes.

"Success, success," she screamed, although I could tell she was trying her best to soften her voice. "This book, American dream, success, rich and famous, you." She thrust the book toward my chest.

I backed up a step, amused by the way she talked to me. In order to persuade me to buy the book, she purposely spoke broken English.

"*Se mun, se mun,* cheap, on sale, American dream, success, rich and famous, only *se mun,* just for you."

It took me quite a while before I realized what she was doing. She had learned to say the price in Cantonese: *se mun*—ten bucks. She had quickly identified me as a new Chinese immigrant, and assumed that I spoke the Cantonese dialect.

I burst out laughing. This was too much, too bizarre, a white American selling the American dream in Cantonese and broken English to a poor Chinese woman. She took my laugh for encouragement and grasped my wrist.

"Yes, American dream, have one."

"Ouch!" I shouted, and tore myself away from her icy grip. How could anyone with such burning eyes have such cold hands, I wondered, as I ran around searching for BMT. There were signs everywhere for N, R, A, E, C, 1, 2, 3, 7, and signs for

Port Authority and the shuttle, but I saw nothing resembling what I needed. Somehow I was back again in the corridor to the 7 train. The smell of the yellow streaks of dried urine along the wall made me sick. I turned quickly into a lane with a sign for N and R. Ghost! It was her again, leaning on the column with the book of the American dream pressed against her chest. How familiar the gesture was! I used to hold onto Mao's book like this, and I used to believe in having beliefs, too.

Three months ago, I left behind everything I had in Shanghai— my lover, my job at Fudan University, my apartment and the books I'd accumulated for ten years, my family and friends— and came to New York to study English and American literature at Brooklyn College. Everyone congratulated me except for Waipo.

"How could you throw away things so lightly?" she asked. "Twelve years ago, you went to the countryside and worked hard in order to get into college. Now you're teaching in one of the best universities in the country and have a nice apartment on the campus. What else do you want? And what about your Ming? You love each other, don't you? How could you leave him just like that? Don't you ever want to have a family? You're twenty-seven, not young anymore. You can't wander around for the rest of your life, Seaweed. I'm really worried."

I poured a cup of hot tea for Waipo and tried my best to comfort her. But fantasies had bloated my brain so much that I had no room to let Waipo's words seep into my consciousness. Even when I arrived at JFK Airport with twenty-five dollars in my pocket, I had never doubted for a second that my new life would be full of excitement, opportunities, and freedom. The next day, my sponsor drove me to 14th Street and put me to work in a branch store of his Oriental antique rug business. I didn't know how to answer the telephone, how to deal with customers; I didn't even know what UPS was. There was no one in that stuffy, moldy store to help me. After a month, my sponsor introduced me to his friends; one owned a restaurant in Flushing, another in midtown Manhattan. He made arrangements with them: I would work as a waitress in the Flushing restaurant on weekends, and in the midtown restaurant I'd pack lunch orders in the kitchen from twelve to three, Monday through Friday, four dollars an hour, so that I could go to my classes at Brooklyn College in the evening. My salary, which would start after the second week, would be approximately five to six hundred dollars a month. I could live on that if I rented a cheap room, my sponsor declared. His wife handed me a Chinese newspaper in which she had circled some rooms for rent in Brooklyn. When I found a place in Bay Ridge for $185 a month, I moved out with my simple luggage and the two hundred dollars my sponsor had lent me for the first month's rent. I felt cheated and abandoned as I lay wide-awake on the floor that night.

Not by my sponsor. I had only gratitude toward him and his wife. He had paid for my trip to America and my first semester's tuition, had let me stay in his place for a month, and had found me these two jobs. Even though it was understood that I would pay him back someday, he still had done me many favors. I really had nothing to complain about concerning him. Who had cheated me then? The American dream? I thought I had risen above that level. I thought I had come here to pursue spiritual liberation. Why was I still depressed when I had the freedom to do anything I wanted? Apparently my motivation wasn't pure enough.

The shuttle came. Harried passengers dispersed quickly in different directions. The woman plucked up her spirit and walked into the crowd, waving her book in the hope of catching someone's eye. "Secret to success. Big sale! Only ten dollars!" she shouted with an authentic New York accent to every passenger who passed her by. Not a single person stopped at her stand. Soon the plaza was empty and quiet again. The woman paced back and forth between two columns, one hand in her pocket, the other still clutching the book. The thin forlorn shadow of her existence finally drew out the tears that I'd been holding back. I cried for her disappointment and sorrow as well as my own. She must be, like me, hungry and exhausted and desperate. We were a pair of ghosts—unseen, unwanted, trapped in this underworld labyrinth.

Footsteps from behind. I turned and saw a young man. "Please, sir, where's BMT?" I quickly wiped my eyes and asked.

"BMT? Cross the plaza, turn right, and you'll see the sign for R and N. Don't follow that. You should turn down the corridor next to the sign on the left, go down some stairs. I'm confusing you, ain't I?" He stopped and noticed my wet cheeks. "Hey, let me take you there. Come with me." He moved toward the plaza. I had no time to hesitate. As we passed the stand, I glanced over his shoulders at the orange book. It was L. Ron Hubbard's *Dianetics*.

The 7 train pulled into its final stop—Times Square. The door opened, but only a few passengers stepped out. The rest sat with ease and amusement, watching the passengers on the platform pushing into the doors and fighting for the few remaining seats. Apparently, those who had seats had taken the previous train for Flushing at the terminal, gotten off at the next stop on Fifth Avenue, and taken the train back to Times Square. In this way, they could get seats for this slow, tiresome trip from Times Square to Flushing.

"Shit, I should have thought of that," I muttered to myself as I struggled to get near the door. A huge woman shoved me from behind. I stumbled into the train, blindly groping for anything to get my balance back. A man grabbed my arm. I was about to say "Thank you, sir," when he moved his hand to my breast and squeezed it as hard as he could before he withdrew quickly with a big smile. The words froze on the tip of my tongue then came out as angry curses, "Shit! Shit! Shit!"

The passengers looked at me as if I was nuts. They had seen this poor guy give me a hand when I was going to fall. And now they saw me cursing him for his help. But how could I explain that he had also given me an unwanted hand on my breast?

"*Kuai lai, kuai lai ya!*" I heard a woman calling in Mandarin. I looked in her direction. She was waving at me through the crowd, her right hand pressing firmly on the empty seat to claim its ownership. "Hurry, hurry, I saved a seat for you," she said in Mandarin again. I looked around in dismay. This woman was a total stranger to me. Maybe she was talking to someone else. But I only saw East Indians, Latinos, African Americans, and a few white men standing around in the car. A group of Koreans sat at one end talking and laughing loudly. It seemed that I was the only person who could understand Mandarin. I pushed through the crowd and sat down next to her.

"Help yourself." She immediately handed me a bag of honey-roasted peanuts. A small box of Christmas gifts sat on her lap.

"Ah, thanks, but I'm not hungry." I swallowed my saliva to suppress the desire to grab some nuts from the bag. I had only enough time to gobble down a cup of hot-and-sour soup in the restaurant where I worked before I rushed to school at three o'clock. Now it was almost ten, and there was nothing in the refrigerator at home. I took out *Tristram Shandy*, trying to shun the delicious smell that stirred up my stomach.

"Ai, life is a nuisance," she sighed heavily, her mouth filled with peanuts, "and marriage is a trap." I looked up from my book and met her gazing eyes. I couldn't tell whether she was young or middle-aged. Her skin still seemed smooth and elastic, but deep lines were permanently carved into her forehead, around her mouth and eyes.

"I envy you, so young and independent. Let me tell you something. Never trust men. They're all scoundrels. Really, I've learned that from my own experience."

I squirmed under her intense gaze, not knowing what to say to her. She threw a few peanuts into her mouth and continued, "I used to be beautiful. Every doctor in the hospital at Taipei where I worked as a nurse ran after me like crazy. See," she rolled up her sleeve, "my skin is still white and soft. I could choose anyone I wanted. But I met Chen in the emergency room. He had acute gastritis from too much drinking and eating at banquets. He was so good-looking, so well dressed, so different from the men I had seen in Taiwan. I took special care of him. When he recovered, he told me he was from New York. We started going to movies and restaurants. Those were the only places you could go in Taiwan. It was so small and crowded. A week later, he presented me with a diamond ring and asked me to marry him. He said he owned a chain of restaurants in Manhattan and Queens and had been looking for someone as beautiful, tender, and capable as me to help him take care of his business. I almost swooned as he put the shiny ring on my finger. I thought I was the luckiest woman in the world. We got married and came to New York. As soon as our honeymoon was over, he put me to work in a restaurant uptown and he himself went off to Atlantic City with his girlfriend. Of course I didn't know what was happening at that time. For seven years, I believed that he was working day and night to keep his restaurants open in a very bad economy. For seven years, I gave him every penny I made. Then one night I came home and found him in bed with another woman. I started screaming and crying. But they just laughed in my face, he and that bitch. He told me everything finally. He was no fucking owner of restaurants, just a sometimes bartender, a sometimes waiter. Yes, he was addicted to gambling and women. My salary had been a big help for his expenses. In that sense, I'd been a good wife. That night I realized what it meant to be heartbroken. He had stolen everything inside me—my heart, my liver, my kidney, my stomach, my brain. I have nothing left. I'm just an empty shell, a body without organs. Ha, ha, ha."

She laughed, but tears dripped on the little green box with the red ribbon.

"Why don't you just walk out?" I said in a harsh tone. I'd been struggling hard to get out of my own depressing situation, and her story certainly didn't help. In fact, my stomach started grumbling again, a sign that I'd soon suffer from gastric pain.

"What?" She jumped and looked at me indignantly. "He's my husband, no matter what he does. Besides, I don't speak English, and I don't know anyone else here. It's fate, you know. I must have done something very bad in my previous life, and I'm now paying for it. It's fate. How can I fight against fate? How can anyone?"

She stared at me hard, but she didn't see me. The blank look gave me goosebumps. I quickly closed my eyes and pretended to doze off.

The train stopped at 90th Street. She stood up, touched my shoulder and said, "Nice to talk to you. Remember what I told you: Don't trust men. Good-bye."

☙

"Hey you, spare me some change," a man spoke behind my back as I was standing on my toes on the edge of the platform of the 7th Avenue Station, stretching my neck to see if the light of the E train had appeared in the dark tunnel.

"What did you say?" I turned around and saw a tall white man, his hand only a few inches from me. He looked to be in his mid-twenties. His long blond hair tangled loosely over his gray, greasy jacket, and his beard curled in profusion over his chest. He was holding a white plastic bag in his other hand. A dirty gray sock spilled out through a hole in its side. "Give me your money, or I'll . . ." he stopped, moving toward me as if he was going to throw me off the platform. His confidence seemed to have risen when he saw an Asian woman. An easy target.

"Ha, I'm being mugged," I said to myself. Funny that I wasn't scared at all. I glanced at the tracks down below, where rats and mice scurried through a litter of empty cans, newspapers, and other garbage soaked in a brownish ooze. Just a few weeks ago, a lunatic had pushed a pregnant woman off the platform of the 34th Street Station. Both the mother and the unborn child had been crushed under the wheels of the D train. What should I do? Cry for help? Plead for mercy? Give him money? Or pull him down onto the tracks to die with me? Suddenly I noticed his hand was trembling. Beads of sweat were rolling down his forehead and nose. He was scared! But I was the one who should be frightened, not the mugger. I tittered. He jumped back, baffled by my laugh.

"Spare me some quarters, please," he said again, his voice now humble and weak.

I took out my purse and poured everything into my hand. There were only six pennies and one nickel. "Sorry, no quarters today," I said with a sincere apology. "Would you take these pennies and the nickel?"

"Sure, sure, I appreciate it." He held out his hand.

"Let's sit down." I pointed to the chairs in the middle of the platform. "Maybe I can find some more in my bag."

We left the dangerous area and sat down next to each other on the plastic chairs. I did find four more pennies and a dime and put everything in his palm. "I wish I could give you more, really, I mean it."

"Thanks, thanks a lot. You tried your best. I appreciate it. Believe me." He poured the coins quickly from his right hand to his left, then from his left to his right, as if they were hot potatoes.

"Why do you do it?"

He jumped, covering the money with both hands. "You mean this?" He made a gesture of juggling the coins.

"No, I mean this." I grasped his hand and held it in a begging gesture. "What a waste! You have such great hands, you know." I traced the lines in his palm with my fingertip. "See this lifeline? It's deep and smooth, and curves nicely. That means you'll live a long, healthy life. Your career line isn't bad either. Only you're too emotional, too indulgent in pleasures. Give me your right hand."

"What for? I don't believe in this witchcraft." But he held out his palm in anticipation.

"I need to see both hands, because the left one only tells what kind of life you were supposed to have. The right one tells how you have altered your fate with your actions."

"I don't want to know it then," he said quickly, trying to withdraw his hand. I gripped his wrist and straightened out his fingers to keep his hand steady. "I can't believe this," I muttered after I had examined his lines. "You have to be very, very careful. Some disaster will take over your body and you may die before you reach thirty. You see this line here? It's broken in the middle. I'm serious. You should really start taking care of yourself. This is not witchcraft."

"Oh my God! Oh, my God!" he howled in a muffled voice, sweat pouring down his face like raindrops. "Why did you do this to me? So it's all written here, I'm doomed. Oh, my God!" He pulled away from me and covered his face with his hands, rocking back and forth while moaning like a wounded animal in a trap.

His reaction scared me. "Come on, you're not taking me serious, are you? You know I was teasing. Of course you're not going to die. You're still young and strong."

I suddenly checked myself. He was still young, but certainly not strong anymore. In fact, I began to notice how ill he was. Fungus had completely eaten into his fingernails. His fingertips were puffed up like dough that had gone sour and then dried. Dark red spots covered his hands, neck, and face. He was skinny and ghostly pale.

He kept whimpering and moaning. "It's true, it's all true. I'm going to die soon, just like my friend. He had AIDS. That horrible disease. Only he was luckier than me. He died in a hospital, in my arms. But I'm going to die on the street, like a dog. Oh my God, my God!"

"I'm so sorry. I didn't know, really," I said, remorseful. "I wish I could help you." I paused for a while, then said, "How about your parents? Do they live in New York? Can they help you?"

"My father threw me out when I told him I was gay. I had no other place to go but my lover's apartment. Then my mother told me that I'd have a bad end. Oh mother's curse! I'm going to die like a dog on the street. Who can help me? Who will help me? Even my own mother cursed me."

He cried, his body collapsed on the seat. A fat black man passed by, dragging behind him a plastic shopping basket. Every few steps he shouted, "Anyone spare me a quarter?" He uttered his last word *quarter* at such a high pitch that it came out as a horrible shriek. The E train came and went. And then another. But I couldn't move an inch, as if his mother's curse had also infected me.

"Guo xin nian, guo xin nian," I murmured to myself to the rhythm of the wheels of the 7 train, my eyes closed so that no one would see my tears. It was the eve of the Spring Festival. If I were in Shanghai, I'd be sitting down at the sixteen-course dinner Waipo had prepared, with my grandpa, my favorite aunts and maybe my parents, sisters, and brother. But right now I had only an empty room to return to. The Elmhurst apartment I shared with three male strangers was infested with rats and roaches. It was after ten o'clock at night. The apartment must be freezing now because the landlady had turned off the heat an hour ago. In order to save oil bills, she heated the apartment only twice a day, from seven to nine in the morning and seven to nine in the evening. I had to wear my down coat, scarf, and gloves in the house.

"Homesick, you, eh?" a man spoke to me in Mandarin with a Taiwanese accent. I opened my eyes reluctantly. He was a good-looking man in his early thirties, although his eyes were bloodshot and his skin a bit dry and blotchy. He wore a stone-washed jean jacket that had at least ten pockets, each of them bulging like a fat baby's cheeks. I smiled as I imagined the kinds of things he put in those pockets.

"My name is Dai." He shook my hand. "Do you know you have a beautiful smile? A little bit sad, but very charming, like a peach blossom in the rain. When my wife, my ex-wife, smiled like that, I'd just go crazy. I felt like I could do anything for her. I wanted to do nothing else but drown in that bewitching smile. Do you understand what I'm talking about? I loved her so much. I gave her everything I had. But she dropped me, just like this—pong!—like a bag of garbage."

"Why did she leave you?" I cut in, not feeling rude at all. He seemed to be the kind of person who could rattle on forever unless interrupted. So far, he hadn't given me a chance to say anything.

"Why? She said I was a liar, a loser. She could waste the rest of her life with a waiter. But I didn't lie. When I courted her in Taiwan, I was the manager of a big corporation. I made a good salary. I took her to fancy restaurants, parties, ballrooms, anywhere she wanted to go. I poured money on her like water. Finally she accepted my proposal, on the condition that I come to New York to further my career. I was terrified. I knew how to manage business, but who would hire a Chinese who hardly spoke English to manage a company in New York? But she wouldn't marry me unless I got the passport. So here I am.

"My brother sponsored me to enter the States. He owns two restaurants. One of them is in Flushing—Uncle Dai's—you must have heard of it. They make the best beef noodles around. Anyway, things were worse than I expected. In the beginning, my brother asked me to manage his restaurant, but I refused. It was too humiliating to work for my brother, who didn't even finish high school in Taiwan. I wanted to start on my own. I looked around for two months but couldn't find a thing. I couldn't even get the lowest job as a delivery boy. When I went back to my brother, he told me he only needed a dishwasher. So this was how I furthered my career: washing dishes twelve hours a day, six days a week, then delivering orders, then serving meals as a waiter.

"Meanwhile, I wrote to her that I was a manager for an import-export company in Flushing, that soon I'd save enough money to buy a house for her. Two years later, she was also granted a visa to immigrate to America. When I took her to the one-bedroom basement in Jackson Heights, she freaked out.

She couldn't stop crying. She couldn't stop cursing me for lying. A week later, she started working in a restaurant too. I couldn't afford keeping her at home, and she couldn't bear being alone in the basement. Three months later, she ran off with the owner of the restaurant. She left me nothing, not even a note."

He closed his mouth all of a sudden, his Adam's apple rolling up and down rapidly to suppress his sobs. I tried to say something to comfort him, but my throat was choked with heaviness.

"I still keep the room the way she liked it," he started talking again. "I hate going home, particularly at night. Would you have dinner with me? I'll take you to the Stone Wok. They have the best fondue. Oh, are you looking for a room? You can stay in my place, you know, rent-free. I work upstate and come home only once a week. You could save a lot of money. Don't be afraid. I won't bother you at all. I'm a nice man. You should see me in a suit and tie. I have a green card. You want to see it?"

"Why do you still stay in New York? You could get a great job in Taiwan," I said gently, trying not to hurt his feelings.

"I told you I have a green card. I've paid dearly for it, the best years of my life. I just couldn't throw it away like that." He unzipped a pocket on his sleeve and took out a laminated light green card. "This piece of paper," he tossed it in his hand and said, "has ruined two people. Sometimes I really want to tear it to pieces and go home."

He sank into silence again. The train stopped at Roosevelt Avenue. I stood up.

"Oh, please, didn't you promise to have dinner with me? Come on, let's go to Flushing."

"Thank you, Mr. Dai. I have to finish a paper for school. Americans don't give holidays for the Spring Festival, you know."

"Oh, oh, leave me your number then. We can have dinner some other time."

"I just moved. I don't have a phone yet."

"Take mine, take mine." He searched his pockets feverishly and found a napkin in his shoulder pouch. I stepped out of the train while he was writing down his phone number. The conductor gave a signal to close the door. Dai rushed forward. The door closed on his shoulders. He screamed. The door opened a little, then shut again. He had only time to pull away his body, his hand, still held between the doors, waving that napkin at me. The train moved, accelerated, and soon disappeared. On the deserted platform, I watched the napkin float here and there in the wind created by the departing subway train.

My
Aunt-in-law

⌒ I woke up this morning thinking of my aunt-in-law. Her image kept coming to me as I leaned on my pillow. I saw her working hard in a laundry or a restaurant in Tokyo, sweating for the amount of money she had dreamed about but had no way of making in China in the early eighties. I saw her drinking with her lover at a bar, her upper body swaying to her favorite jazz music.

I felt ashamed for thinking of her like this, so calm and void of hatred. I was supposed to detest her, because her lust and greed had done much harm to Waipo's and my family.

Last spring, I received a letter from my *waipo*. "Dear granddaughter Seaweed," she said. Waipo, being illiterate, depended on others to write for her. That was why her letters always sounded formal and impersonal.

"Your uncle and aunt divorced. Your aunt went to Japan to study. How are you doing in New York? Please take care of yourself. Eat a lot. Rest well. When can you come back to China?"

I was extremely worried, not about my uncle, but about my grandma. My uncle had caused her so much misery until he married my aunt-in-law. Now that his wife had dumped him, the torture would start again.

No one in Waipo's family liked my uncle. My first memory of him was when he bit my finger to get a cookie from me. It was my third birthday. He was eight. Food was scarce then, and a cookie was the best delicacy one could find. Waipo had bought it on the black market for two yan, which was 15 percent of Waigong's monthly salary. My uncle had tried to trade the cookie for his toys, and when he saw that I was determined to hold onto my birthday present and was nibbling at it as fast as I could, he grabbed my hand and chomped at the cookie, biting my hand while doing so. Even though Waipo whipped him with a bamboo stick, I still couldn't stop crying for my lost cookie.

Waipo, Mother, and my aunts never talked about my uncle in front of me. Every time I came to Shanghai to visit Waipo, I would often be awakened at midnight as they argued in muffled voices over my uncle. I pretended to be asleep and over-heard all the incredible things he had done. He ran away from school, fought with his bosses, was suspended from jobs, molested neighborhood girls, stole furniture from Grandma and bikes from movie theaters, was beaten up by the gang he was involved with, interrogated by the police, and attempted suicide twice. No one in the family talked to him except Waipo. She cursed him and vowed every day that she would throw him out, but whenever my uncle appeared stealthily at the door, she served him hot meals. My two aunts threatened that they would cut off her monthly allowance if she continued seeing him. Waipo promised and vowed, yet she kept washing his clothes and giving him food when her daughters were not around. Often, when she watched my uncle bring his girlfriend to his room, she would sigh, "Things will be better once he gets married."

My uncle seemed to have a new girlfriend every month. He could attract girls because he was tall and handsome. His naturally tanned skin was just becoming fashionable in Shanghai, and he had bulging muscles in his chest and arms due to his daily exercises. His thick black hair was always carefully combed backward, his shoes always shiny. But he couldn't keep any of the girls. I didn't blame them. Who would want to marry a person like my uncle?

He married in the summer of 1981, very quickly and quietly. Waipo broke the news to me on the day I arrived in Shanghai from Beijing. I hadn't seen her for two years since I left Hangzhou Foreign Language School to study in Beijing Foreign Language Institute. As she was fixing my favorite breakfast— soy sauce noodle soup—on the stove in the hallway, she told me that my uncle had married the month before. The bride was Ying Na.

At first, the name didn't ring a bell. Waipo repeated the name. "Ying Na, Ying Na Liu—you've been to her house."

I couldn't close my mouth. Ying Na, how could it be possible? She was the only daughter of a high-ranking army official, who had a house in the best area in Shanghai, a house with a garden. She knew my uncle through her fifth brother, and befriended my little sister, Sea Gull, who was then living with Waipo. I met Ying Na only once, in 1975, during a short visit in Shanghai. I was still working as a farmer in Lishao. Sea Gull took me to her house one evening. A maid opened the iron gate and let us in without saying a word. Through the glass wall, I saw the family sitting around the dining room table—six young men and a young woman. An old woman was serving noodles to an old man at the head of the table. He was the only one who was eating and talking; his audience listened with obvious boredom on their faces. The dining room was decorated with exotic-looking plants and flowers, antique jars and vases, and many paintings on the walls, and there was a spiral staircase in the back.

Ying Na was delighted to see us. It gave her an excuse to leave the table and her father's lecture. She showed us around the house. I was shocked that she and her five brothers each had their own bedrooms. I didn't have my own bed until I was fifteen, when I left home and went to the countryside to be a farmer. As we sat in Ying Na's snow white room, I hid my legs under the chair, wishing I could also cover my face somehow. My skin had not only become dark brown but had also chapped and blistered from being exposed to the summer sun twelve to fourteen hours a day in the rice fields. I was relieved that nobody talked to me. I watched with admiration Ying Na's energetic and elegant movements. She wasn't stunningly beautiful, but vitality and confidence radiated through her powerful legs and waist. I was awed by her manner and that environment.

"How are your noodles, Seaweed?" Waipo asked as she watched me eating. "When you finish, I want you to visit your aunt and uncle. You should see their bridal room. It's really something."

My uncle lived in the room beneath Grandma's, between the second and third floors. Built for storing things, it was only about eight meters square, with a small window facing the public water pump. I used to hate going into that damp stinky room. Now I was curious about how Ying Na had adjusted to this dungeon. The door opened before I knocked. For a moment, I thought I had walked into the wrong place.

"Welcome, college student," my uncle said smoothly, holding the door for me.

What a surprise! My uncle had never acted so politely to me, or to anybody. And it was the first time I had ever heard him say a complete sentence without stuttering. He unfolded a chair and poured a cup of iced tea from a flask.

"Have a drink, Seaweed. Your aunt will be back at any moment."

I held the glass with both of my hands, too shocked to say a word. Since when had he become such a gentleman?

I looked around the room. A queen-sized bed took up almost half the space. A twenty-four-inch color TV sat on top of a dressing table between the wall and the bed, along with an assortment of cosmetics: lipsticks, blush, Vella Shampoo, and hair conditioner. A closet stood in the corner where the toilet used to be, with a large red paper cutting of the character Happiness on the mirror, a symbol of marriage. It was a miracle that such a small room could hold so many things and still have space for a few chairs. My uncle turned on the TV. Beautiful pictures. My parents had a set that produced glaring white lines on the dark background and hissing noises. They put a piece of special plastic on the screen to make it colorful, but it only turned the pictures into an awful shade of purple. Uncle was the first one in the family to own a TV, and the first one to own a color TV. "It's a Sony," he said proudly, "the best brand on the market." His next goal was to get a remote control TV and a VCR.

Someone was coming upstairs, the footsteps steady and powerful. The door opened. Ying Na came in with a casserole. "Welcome, college student." Her warm, broad smile broke the awkward moment of the changed relationship. I called her Ying Na instead of aunt. She asked me many questions about Beijing Foreign Language Institute. She said she loved English and was taking lessons from the radio and TV. It might come in handy someday. She talked on and on, the echoes of her clear voice bouncing around the smooth walls of that eight-meter-square room as if looking for an exit.

I noticed her thick waist. When I went upstairs, I asked Waipo about it. She hushed me with a finger on her lips and whispered in my ear—six months already. When her parents found out before the wedding that she was four months' pregnant, they were so furious that they disowned her. They even refused to come to the wedding. Wow! I stuck out my tongue. Her courage to marry my uncle under such pressure was admirable. But secretly I still felt it was a pity that she married such a bum.

"Where did they get the money for the TV and the furniture?" I asked. If Ying Na's family disowned her, they wouldn't give her money. It was impossible to get those things with their meager salaries. Waipo gestured at me to lower my voice. "Your uncle has a clothing stand on the Huaihai Street. Money comes in every day. It's legal. Your aunt got a license for him through her friends. It's good. I don't have to worry like when he was a scalper, buying and selling movie tickets, bicycles, and TV ration tickets to make money. I never expected that your uncle, a good-for-nothing, could marry such a nice girl. Did you notice how he has changed? He even gave me that." She pointed to an old nine-inch black-and-white TV. "Remember the way he used to steal from me and caused all that trouble?"

I read Waipo's letter several times, trying to find out more details between the few lines. I knew Waipo didn't want to let an outsider or her grandchildren learn anything bad about our family. She would have told me in person, but I was thousands of miles away. The only person who would give me the information now was my mother.

I waited for a month. When the letter finally came, I let it sit on my desk for a week before I gathered enough courage to open it. "Seaweed," she wrote. She used to call me Wang Haizao. Since I came to America, she started calling me by my given name.

Your *waipo* must have told you that your aunt-in-law divorced your uncle and went to Japan as a student. She gave your uncle twenty thousand yuan as a condition to get a divorce. He became involved with two prostitute sisters soon after she left. The two prostitutes slept with him together, one sucked his penis while the other licked his balls. They stayed with him until he spent the last fen of the divorce money. When they stopped visiting him, he went to their apartment and beat them up, breaking one girl's ribs. The sisters have relatives in the local police station. They arrested him and gave him two years in jail. Their son Mo is living with me now. Poor child! First he lost his mother, who has never written him one word since she left, then his father, and his maternal grandparents don't want to have anything to do with him. Your grandparents are too old to take care of him. Your uncle and aunts planned to send him to the countryside, where it's much cheaper to raise a child. I was furious. Shen Mo is the only son in our family to carry on the name. How could he be treated like this? I took him to Dinghai without consulting your father. Poor old man, he's very unhappy, of course, and jealous. It's so disgraceful, the way your aunt deserted your uncle and her son to seek luxury with her lover. It's a shame and tragedy on our Shen family. I'm surprised that I still have the energy and patience to bring up another child after all the years with my own four children. Well, I guess I don't have any other choice but to take on the responsibility as the eldest daughter of the Shen family.

I quickly put the letter in my drawer, trying to forget it. Why did my mother give me all the details? Things must have been very bad if she had to take care of the little child. How impatiently she had waited for her own children's independence so she could have a few years of freedom and fun before she got too old! We all learned to take care of ourselves and share the household chores at around five years old, including my brother, Sea Tiger, the only son. We all did our own laundry. Father did most of the daily shopping for food. Nainai cooked, and after she left, I took over the job. I washed the dishes, and Sea Cloud and Sea Tiger cleaned the table and swept the floor after the meals. So there wasn't much left for Mother to do. Still, her favorite talk was about the good and peaceful life she would lead when we all left home and sent her a monthly allowance.

I was relieved that my mother took him in. The poor boy needed attention and protection.

Mo was two and a half when I first met him. I was going to New York to study American literature and made a special trip to Shanghai to say good-bye to my grandparents. When I asked my grandma about my baby cousin and the parents, she said they were fine, but her expression changed. I went to knock on their door. Ying Na opened it angrily. She was all dressed up: short leather skirt, black net stockings, highheeled black shoes, her hair permed into small short curls. Her face had also been carefully painted. Everything she wore was imported and could be purchased only on the black market at high prices. My uncle sat on the bed with the baby howling for his mother. He had nothing on but a pair of shorts. Apparently they were having a fight. Ying Na pulled me into the room, made me sit down on the chair, and poured me a glass of Chinese cola from the refrigerator. The child stopped crying when he saw his mother come back, and my uncle heaved a sigh of relief. Ying Na kept congratulating me for going abroad, and made me tell her all the details about the process of getting a passport and visa. She listened, her eyes sparkling with hope and envy and determination. Then she said firmly and clearly, as if announcing a decision, "I'm learning Japanese. I'm planning to go to Japan to study." She was so serious that I dared not laugh. She had only a high school diploma. What could she study over there? What about her family? The baby started crying again. He was named Mo, meaning silence, yet his wailing was so loud that my head hurt. My aunt took him in her arms, and touched his chin with her finger, ignoring the child's saliva, which was dripping on her blouse.

"Isn't he cute?" she said proudly. "He weighed four and a half kilograms when he was born, almost killed me. Look at his big earlobes, a sign of good luck. I wish his good luck would help me get a visa."

The baby did look very healthy, red cheeks, big eyes, and a square chin like my uncle's. But his eyes had a hungry look, and his hands waved around in the air nervously as if grabbing something to hold on to.

"Are you all prepared?" she asked me. "What are you going to take with you?" I told her I wanted to buy a thick warm sweater in Shanghai. Did she know where I could get a good one? "Don't waste your time and energy. There's nothing good, nothing really good," she said. "When are you leaving? Let me knit one for you. It'll be your dream sweater." I told her I was leaving in two days. She pressed my arms and said, "Listen, I'm going out to a party. I'll buy the yarn on my way and start it when I come back. Just tell me what color and style, and by the day after tomorrow you'll have a sweater." I looked at her, then at her son, and last at my uncle. For the first time her eyes fell on him. "I'm going to the party alone. It's a dancing party. I have my own partner. He's great. If your uncle could dance half as well as him, I would let him go with me. But, you know your uncle—he can't even say a sentence smoothly. I really have to run. Stay a bit longer if you want. You have such great eyebrows and lips, only they need a little plucking and color. I'll fix them for you when I get back. Bye-bye."

She closed the door behind her. The child was howling again and crawling to the edge of the bed. My uncle shrugged his shoulders helplessly. "This room is too small for her," he said.

Dayi told me later that my aunt-in-law was having an affair with her dancing partner. My uncle went to the school where his wife worked and broke into her desk with an ax. He found all the love letters the guy had written to her. They were planning to go to Japan together. My uncle showed the letters to the head of the school, who took my aunt-in-law's position away from her and ordered her to work in the school factory while undergoing self-criticism. It had been three months. She could have started teaching again if she had admitted her mistake, but she refused to repent.

Repent? I recalled the short encounter with Ying Na and could only remember how excited she was about going to a party. I don't think she has ever repented for anything she has done.

Ying Na kept her promise though. She knitted me a beautiful sweater: light purple, big sleeves, low neck. It opened like a butterfly when I stretched my arms. It was the only presentable piece of clothing I owned when I first arrived in New York. Unfortunately it shrank to the size of a baby sweater when I put it in the washing machine, and I had to give it to the Salvation Army.

A few months later, I received a letter from my father. I weighed it in my hand. It was thick and heavy. Since I left home at fifteen, my father had written to me only once. That was when I lost my job because of my plans to go abroad to study, and was sleeping in the subways and train stations of Beijing. He sent me some rice ration coupons and money, and told me to do what I thought was right. This was his first letter since I came to America. My mother had been communicating with me, but she rarely mentioned my father's name. I opened the letter.

Tears came out as I read "Daughter Seaweed." It made me realize how much I had longed to hear from him.

> Your mother is bewitched by that little boy, that little monster, Mo. She buys him anything he wants. When I come home from work, I often have to eat leftovers or nothing at all. If I complain, they both laugh at me and tell me to stop drinking or smoking so that I can save some money for decent food. But I know what they eat while I'm not home. I've seen the bones of chickens and fish in the dustbin. The little boy is a devil. He pours my liquor into the sink and fills the bottle with pee and water. Once he put a firecracker in my cigarette. When it exploded and burnt my nose, your mother didn't punish him at all. She even said it should teach me a lesson and help me quit smoking. The boy steals. He started stealing from me, then your mother. He steals anything—money, rice coupons, clothing, small pieces of furniture, things he can sell. Once he took four hundred jin worth of rice coupons from our neighbor and sold them for fifty yuan. By the time your mother found out, he had spent it all. Guess how he spent the money? First he took a rickshaw to school, then he took his class out for ice

cream, and finally he gave the rest of the money to three boys who were willing to serve him and call him master. He's just like your uncle and your ex-aunt-in-law. What do you expect? A product of two jerks.

Your mother wouldn't admit it, although she searches him before he leaves for school in the morning. No matter what he does, she believes he's the best child in the world. She even refuses to sleep in the same bed with me, saying that I snore too much. But the real reason is that she wants to sleep with that little devil. It hurts so much as I lay in bed listening to their talking and laughing. I often wonder if this is still my home, if that woman is still my wife, for whom I've worked so hard. I'm fifty-two years old. I've raised four children, two of them are college graduates. I thought I could live the rest of my life peacefully and comfortably. But I have nothing. He even stole my radio—my only property after thirty-five years of work.

I wish you could write to your mother and make her see what she's doing. But I guess nothing can wake her up until the little devil destroys her completely. Sometimes I really feel sorry for him. It's all his mother's fault. I'm thinking of getting a divorce. I can't go on like this any more.

Yours,
Father

I buried my head in my arms on the keyboard of the computer in the kitchen and sat there for a long time. My boyfriend asked me several times, each time more irritably, what was the matter. I just remained silent until he became furious and walked out, slamming the door behind him. I had to bear the pain and shame alone. He might sympathize for a moment, but he would never understand, and during our next fight he might use it as a weapon against me.

I didn't write to my mother. She was beyond my power. Even now, though I was thousands of miles away from her, I still trembled when I got her letters. It was as if she were standing at the door with a bamboo stick in her hand, waiting to punish me. I sent my father a hundred dollars. Buy yourself a record player, I wrote, and use it in your office.

I didn't hear from him again. But I knew he got the money, because my mother's letters were full of complaints about how things were getting more expensive day by day, and how poor her health was. My father must have bought another radio and showed off his new possession. I didn't send her any money, though. She shouldn't be in need of money. Since I came to America, I had mailed her two hundred dollars every Chinese New Year—one hundred for her, one hundred for my father. But I was sure she never gave my father a penny. Two hundred dollars represented my parents' combined annual salary. Now she could afford a chicken once a week.

I never dreamed that letter would be my father's last communication with me. About a year later, Sea Cloud called me at four o'clock in the morning. Father was dead. Liver cancer. It was quick, only a month from the discovery of the disease to his death. "Up to the last moment, he still asked for medicine," my sister sobbed over the phone. He had never believed he was going to die. He was only fifty-three.

The Immigration Department had just granted me a green card three weeks before. I could go back to China for my father's funeral without worrying whether China would give my passport back and whether the u.s. Embassy would reissue my visa. Sea Cloud went to Shanghai to meet me. We stayed in Waipo's place before we took a ship to Dinghai. There I met Mo again. He was doing his homework at the dinner table. He stood up immediately when we entered the room, and ran to meet us. He called me Sister Seaweed. I saw the obvious combination of my uncle and Ying Na in his face. I was looking for the demon in his handsome eyes, but all I saw was warmth and excitement. And he had such perfect manners. He brought me a pair of slippers, then a basin of hot water with a clean towel in it. Before I finished wiping my face, he handed me a jar of moisture lotion. I had hated him for torturing my father in his last year of life, but when I left, I gave him the video game I had planned to give my brother as a present.

Sea Cloud sulked the whole night on the ship, no matter how often I asked her what was the matter. Finally she asked me why I was so nice to Mo. "Do you know how he tortured our father?" she asked. "He practically killed him. If not for him, Father wouldn't have drunk so much. He stole from him and turned Mother against him. Father became lonely and angry. No one in the family spoke to him. When he tried to talk, everybody just laughed. They had all been bewitched by that little monster.

"I didn't realize the situation in the beginning," she said sadly. "When I found out, it was already too late. Father had been diagnosed as having liver cancer. He had nobody to turn to." My sister looked at the sea and avoided my eyes. She was crying again. "So all his anger and misery accumulated in his liver. Mother still tried to keep the boy, but Brother and I told her that if she didn't send him back to Shanghai, she'd never see us again. So Father, in his last moments, helped us to get rid of him."

I recalled Mo's round rosy cheeks and his polite smile as he listened to Waipo lecturing him. I just couldn't think of him as a monster. Would he be a normal child if his mother hadn't had the affair, or divorced his father, or gone to Japan? But why shouldn't she go to Japan if she had a chance? Why shouldn't she divorce my uncle if she wasn't happy with him? I'd known from the beginning that their relationship wouldn't last long.

As if reading my mind, my sister said, "Our uncle is a jerk, but so is our aunt-in-law. Mo is the product of a couple of jerks. You'll agree with me after you spend three months with the boy."

My mother didn't change much except that she had a big stomach. She still talked, cursed, and walked fast and loud. She had arranged everything for the funeral, even sewed my father a new jacket, a pair of pants, and a cap—all made of silk. My father had shrunk to the size of an eight-year-old child. My sister told me he couldn't eat in his last month. After he was cremated, I poured a glass of cognac—the most expensive kind I could get in New York—over his ashes. I had promised him, when I left China, that I'd bring him back the best liquor in the world.

Everything went smoothly. All the Wang family members were present at the funeral. And all of Father's colleagues came with flowers. Soon my ten-day leave was up. On the eve of my departure, the family sat together, chatting casually. My brother and sisters were content because I had promised to help them to come to America on the condition that they learn some English. Mother also wanted to "take a look at New York" before she was too old to move around. I told her to wait a few years. Once I was naturalized by the Immigration Department, she could visit me any time she wanted. We talked about the different ways of learning English, about how to find partners to practice with. "It's not hard to find a partner nowadays," Sea Tiger said. "The whole nation is learning English because everyone wants to go abroad. Even our uncle is learning English in jail."

We all became quiet at the mention of his name. He was going to be let out in eight months. What was he going to do? What about his son? Would he take him back or let him stay with his grandparents? The air became very tense. My mother stopped smiling and moved her needles swiftly; she was knitting a sweater for me. My brother started talking about the naughty things our cousin Mo had done, thinking they might make us laugh. Before Mo left for Shanghai, he had soiled every bed, making sure that he got each corner and edge. It took Mother and Sea Cloud weeks to clean them thoroughly and get rid of the shit and the smell. We all laughed. "What a sly brat," Mother said, her tone full of love and indulgence. "Like father, like son," Sea Tiger added.

"What's wrong with our Shen family?" Mother threw her knitting materials on the floor, pointing her finger at Sea Tiger's nose. "What's wrong with your uncle and cousin? Nothing. They're smarter than all of your Wang family members put together." She swept her hand to include Sea Cloud, Sea Tiger, Sea Gull, and me. "They're just ruined by that bitch Ying Na. Why are you sitting here laughing at the unfortunate, Wang Haizao? You can go anywhere you want since you have a green card. Why didn't you go to Japan to condemn your aunt-in-law, to tell her to write to her son and send him some money? Like father, like son, eh?" she pointed at Sea Tiger again. "Exactly. Look at yourself—what have you accomplished at the age of twenty-eight? Are you going to be a shop assistant all your life? Are you going to be an alcoholic like your father? Ha! Like father, like son."

A year had passed since I came back to New York from China, and I could still hear my mother's angry voice. But every time I tried to turn my grief for my father's death and Mo's abnormal behavior into hatred for my aunt-in-law, I'd see Ying Na's frustrated eyes and hear her say, "I must go. I must!"

She told me this at our last meeting, when she came upstairs to Waipo's room to give me the sweater she knit overnight. We went to the balcony together because she didn't want to enter the room. As we were chatting, we noticed our neighbors were peeking at us from their windows.

"They're staring at me," Ying Na sneered, "but I don't give a damn." She looked directly into my eyes. "You must have heard of what your uncle did to me at my school. I'm being punished for having a lover. But will he ever be punished for invading my privacy and breaking my property? Never!" She turned and spat at the windows. "I can't take it anymore. To tell you the truth, I married your uncle just to defy my father. I'd rather die than marry a man he had chosen for me, to live all my life in one of the rooms in his house." She looked around as if she were trapped in a pit. "All your uncle can think of is how to expand the clothing stand so he can buy a vcr. But who cares if he gets a hundred vcrs. Life should be more than having a vcr, a small room, a husband, and a child. I envy you, Seaweed." She grabbed my arms with her trembling hands. "You've a college degree and can go abroad on your own. I sleep with Lee, my lover, not only because I don't love your uncle anymore, but also because he can take me to Japan. How I wish I could go right now! Whenever I think of spending all my life in this dungeon and the fucking elementary school, I feel so sick that I want to set fire to everything. I don't believe that it's a paradise out there. But at least I'll have the freedom to choose what I want to do. Even if I become a waitress, a laundry woman or a whore, it'll be my own choice."

Lying on my bed, I noticed, from the calendar on the wall, that it was the anniversary of Father's death. Mother should have received the fifty dollars she asked for. She wanted to hire a monk to read some scripture for Father's soul. She didn't mention my uncle and Mo in her letters. That meant things were okay with them. She no longer talked about having me fly to Tokyo to condemn Ying Na. Maybe she had realized that it was beyond my power. Beyond anyone's power.

Fox
Smell

⌒ I have scars in the shape of maple leaves on each of my armpits.

My Chinese boyfriends, being polite and considerate, pretended not to see them. The scars indicated that I had had an operation to get rid of the odor in my armpits—the fox smell. It was a shame, a girl with the fox smell.

My American boyfriends were fascinated by them. Oriental scars on the armpits. One liked to inspect them before and after sex, licking them, squeezing out the dirt that hid between the creases. One asked endless questions. What happened? Why, when, and where? One day, in a Moroccan restaurant where we had taken his friend Nick to celebrate his sixtieth birthday, my friend asked me to lift my arms to show Nick the scars. "They are amazing, really amazing," he told Nick in a proud tone, as if he had won a six-number lottery.

I pulled a long face and said, "Why don't you show Nick your asshole."

Silence. Nick was gay. They called each other sweetie.

I raised my voice, "I said, why don't you show Nick your asshole."

My boyfriend kicked at the table and threw a fit. He refused to look at or talk to me for a whole week.

For many years I couldn't explain why and when I got the scars. Not true. I remembered exactly what had happened. But I didn't want to. I tried to forget. I tried to hide.

First it was to hide the stench that came involuntarily from the armpits—stubborn and strong, like the growth of my breasts. I washed ten times a day, pulled the hair out of the armpits, and covered the areas with musk and tiger-bone plasters. Nothing worked. The medicine in the plasters stimulated the blood circulation and made the smell even worse. Only a miracle could save me now, I said to myself. The content of my prayer changed from making me as pretty and smart as Sea Cloud into making me smell no more.

The odor is called *hu chou* in Chinese—fox smell. I've never seen a real fox so I can't say if I smelled like a fox at that time. But I always connected the odor with overnight chicken shit, rotten onions, and dead snails. These three things are associated with my sister's discovery of my fox smell.

Seven o'clock in the morning I was cleaning chicken shit out of the bathroom. I raised twelve chickens, eleven hens for eggs and one rooster for mating. There was a shed in the backyard, but Mother said it wasn't safe outside at night. People stole chickens, and so did yellow weasels. So the chickens spent their evenings in the bathroom and two more chores were added to my heavy morning duties—to let out the chickens and clean up after them. The first one was a big headache. Our apartment was like a train, one room after another. Since the bathroom was in the back, the chickens had to go through the kitchen, the children's room, and my parents' room, which led to the outside world. They were curious animals who did not like to follow directions. They loved to dive into the corners, under the beds and tables, sometimes to chase a roach, sometimes simply to have some fun. I wouldn't have minded their playfulness if I didn't have other morning chores or a strict order from Mother that she must never be disturbed when she was asleep. It became an important issue to choose the right moment to let out the chickens. Too early, Mother would be awakened; too late, Mother wouldn't have a clean bathroom. Fortunately it took her about ten minutes to wake up. During the ten minutes, she stretched, yawned, cleared her throat, talked to Father, sometimes even hummed a song. It gave me just enough time to take out the chickens and clean up the bathroom.

So on that hot August morning, I had just finished scooping the chicken shit into a dustpan with a small shovel and was about to wash the cement floor when Sea Cloud entered the bathroom. She passed by me and started sniffing around.

"It's the chicken shit," I snapped before she opened her mouth. She had just gotten up, her hair uncombed, her eyes still half closed, whereas I'd been up for two hours, walked two miles to and from the market to shop for the day's food, lit the coal stove, cooked the breakfast, and let out the chickens. What right did she have to pick on me now? Didn't like the smell? Too bad! Get up earlier and clean it yourself, I said to her in my head. That was all I could do. If I had said it out loud, Sea Cloud would have run to Mother and had me punished.

"Not that, something else, on you," Sea Cloud said in her sweet, unsuspicious voice, her pink slender finger pointing at me.

I threw the hose on the floor and examined my clothes. Why was I so careless? I had stained myself again with the chicken shit. Damn, I had enough chores as it was. I really didn't want to wash my shirt again. Sweat poured down my forehead and cheeks. I lifted my arm to wipe my face with my sleeve.

"Your armpits, your armpits," Sea Cloud shouted and covered her nose with a handkerchief. *"Hao chou!"*

Very stinky, a free translation of *hao chou*. The literal meaning is good *(hao)* and smelly *(chou)*. Does it mean that it's good to be smelly or that a good smell makes stink? To describe something bad with a complimentary word just doesn't make sense. But words are never reasonable. Words contradict themselves constantly.

My arm was still lifted in the air. A strange, pungent smell assailed my nostrils as Sea Cloud uttered *hao chou*. It was so strong that I stopped breathing for a moment. My head spun and exploded like popcorn . . . all the blood gone . . . nothing for the brain . . . *hao chou* . . . shame . . . when I resumed my breathing, the smell stayed in my nose, my mouth, my stomach . . . as if I had just swallowed a lump of chicken shit and it stuck in my throat . . . no in . . . no out . . .

Sea Cloud backed out of the bathroom. I banged the door shut and turned on the shower. The cold water washed my body . . . my clothes . . . my soul . . . if I still had one . . . I wouldn't blame it if it had escaped . . . who wanted to be in this stinky shell . . . I was standing in the chicken shit . . . I was the chicken shit . . . *hao chou* . . .

I went through the morning routine as usual, serving breakfast, washing dishes, and cleaning vegetables for lunch. The chores had never seemed so endless and boring. I peeled one layer of the onion, rotten. Another layer, still rotten. Rotten to the heart. I picked the fifth one. These onions had been forgotten for too long. They were shrunken, like Nainai's cheeks. But there must be one I could use to sauté with the sliced potato for lunch. Potato with onion. It would be better if there were some sliced pork. The Russians believed that Communism equaled potatoes and beef stew once a day. What about potatoes with onion? Was it Socialism? Ten minutes till twelve. Mother was coming home at any moment. The soup and two other dishes were on the table. The oil was burning on the stove. Another rotten heart. What did it smell like? No, I smelled nothing. My nose had been closed since morning.

That sniffing sound again . . . behind my back . . . something smelled funny . . . I chopped the onion with all my strength . . . juice splashing . . . *hao chou* . . . I turned around . . . knife in my hand . . . Sea Cloud stood there . . . her eyes narrowed . . . her nostrils wrinkled . . . her lips pouted and turned upwards . . . a pinched face . . . but still beautiful . . . like the face of a fox . . . seductive and merciless . . .

"*Hu chou,*" she said quietly, without looking at me, as if she was muttering in her own dream.

"What?" I asked, although I heard it clearly. She walked away without answering, her pigeonlike chuckles echoing against the walls of the kitchen.

Hu chou—fox smell. This was what I had, in my armpits. How did Sea Cloud know? Mother told her? God's arrangement: she had the fox face, me the fox smell. I sank my face into my collar. The smell of rotten onions rose from the dark, furry pits. Although my first period hadn't yet come, parts of my body were already covered with thick hair. It had given me a good scare when I first discovered the hair on my legs and pubic area, thinking I had turned into a man. I took a deep breath. I must get used to this stench. This was part of me.

I didn't join my family for lunch. No one asked for me or called me to the table; they were used to my absence. Most of the time they started eating while I was still cooking. By the time I sat down, they'd already finished their meals. I was pissed off in the beginning, but now I liked it. When I ate alone, I could do whatever I wanted; I could read a book or listen to the radio and no one would tell me that it was bad for digestion. That day I went to the bathroom when my family sat down for lunch. I squatted over the toilet pit and opened Pu Song Ling's *Liaozhai zhiyi*. The book was full of stories about how female fox spirits or ghosts seduced men (usually scholars), then sucked their yang, or blood, from the bottom of their feet. But if the scholars could resist the temptation, the fox spirits and ghosts would fall in love with them and helped them get rich. The men would then help the fox ghosts become humans, and they would get married, have children, and live happily ever after. All these female fox ghosts were unbelievably beautiful and clever, and excellent in bed.

When I limped out of the bathroom, my family was taking a nap. I ate whatever was left over, cleaned up, then sat down on a stool to clip off the bottoms of the snails with a pair of scissors. No time for me to nap. I had to cut two *jin* of snails for supper. This was not an easy job—all these snails taking up the whole basin. In the water, they all stretched their boneless bodies out of their shells, attaching themselves to one another with their sucking discs. They withdrew into their shells when they felt my touch, as if to escape the fate of being cut up and cooked alive. Mother was a snail expert. She pressed a snail between her lips and sucked, making a noise like the one I heard from her room at night, like the beautiful ghosts sucking the blood from men's feet. Who sucked whom, mother or father? Mother never needed a second try—one suck, and the snail fell into her mouth, naked, helpless. The snails resisted my scissors passively with their hard shells. I felt sorry for them. Nobody deserved to have their bottoms cut off. Nobody deserved to die like this. But I kept clipping, in spite of the blisters on my fingers. I had delayed the lunch, and must make it up with a good supper. Three meals a day, three dishes a meal, this was my life, like mountains weighing on my soul. If I were only a fox spirit! Life seemed to be easy for them: they could get anything they wanted with their magic, except for the thunderclaps that would kill them every five hundred years. And they were all so pretty. What about their smell? *Hu chou*—fox smell. Did I really smell like a fox?

When Sea Cloud stepped out of the bathroom, I had just crushed a snail. It had been dead for days. The shell became crispy and broke into pieces under the pressure of my scissors. The stench of the rotten flesh made Sea Cloud stumble. She missed a step and kicked the basin. If I hadn't grabbed her arms, she would have fallen on the wet cement floor among the scattered snails. Sea Cloud looked up in annoyance, as if her stumble was my fault. Suddenly I saw her face pinch together again. "Boy," she said in utter contempt, shaking off my touch, "you really stink." Then she shouted toward the room where Mother was sleeping, "Mom, tell Seaweed to do something about her armpits."

I don't remember how long I stood among the scattered snails, when Mother took my hands, led me into the bathroom and turned on the shower. I only remember Mother's soft fingers and her gentle touch. Very unusual, as if she were sorry for me, as if my misery were her fault. In the shower, I stared at my blistered bony hands. Mother had once put them next to Sea Cloud's slender white hands and told our fortunes: Sea Cloud was chosen to live a prosperous life whereas I was doomed to lifelong hardship.

This was how I grew up—suddenly and painfully. In the shower, I stared at my hands, at my armpits. *Hao chou . . . hu chou.* Fox spirits and fox smell. Why me? The water poured down on my shoulders, steady like the three meals a day I had to prepare. This stench.

I met Jian Ning at Hangzhou Foreign Language School. She was the first and the only girlfriend I've ever had. I was madly attached to her, never let her out of my sight. I loved her armpits. When we were together, the first thing I would do would be to put my hands in those places. The moisture and warmth made me feel safe. At first Jian Ning giggled and protested that it was ticklish and ridiculous. But gradually she became so used to my habit that whenever she saw me, she would open her arms without thinking, like a hen calling her chicks into her wings. One day, after I warmed up in her armpits, I moved my hands to her belly and began to knead the folds of flesh around her waist. She was a big woman, almost twice my size; her stomach was ample but extremely firm, like the dough used to make noodles. Mother loved homemade noodles, so twice a week, I used to spend the whole afternoon kneading the dough, rolling it out until it was as thin as paper, and cutting it into noodles. I hated doing this with my heart and soul, but kneading Jian Ning's stomach gave me tremendous pleasure. Suddenly she pushed me away and said, "My god, you're a fox spirit, a man eater."

I looked at her in disbelief. Me, a fox spirit? Men never gave me a second look and I hadn't been able to talk to a man for more than five minutes. I was twenty-one, but I'd never gone out with anybody. Me, a man-eater? She must be kidding. But Jian Ning looked serious. Her cheeks flushed with excitement.

"Jian Ning, please don't make fun of me. I'm not a fox spirit, you know that. But it's true I have the fox smell, or used to, but not anymore, I think. I had an operation. Look." As I lifted my arms, tears filled my eyes. I felt vulnerable, standing with my arms above my head, as if I were surrendering myself. Would my scars disgust my only friend?

She covered my armpits with her hands and pressed her cheek against my belly. "It makes no difference. You're still a fox

spirit, or will be. You know Concubine Yang, the one who ruined the greatest emperor in the Tang Dynasty? She wasn't that
beautiful. There were thousands of concubines in the palace
who were much better looking. It was her smell, the fox smell,
that enchanted the emperor. I can tell you many other stories
like this."

I nodded and smiled, happy that my scarred armpits didn't
drive her away, although I couldn't understand why she kept
telling me that I was a fox spirit as if it were a great compliment,
nor could I see the connection between the fox smell and female attraction. If the odor were really as enchanting as Jian
Ning believed, why were there so many posters and ads for
medicine to get rid of the fox smell? And my uncle wouldn't
have gone through several operations, and Waipo wouldn't
have acted like my savior.

A few weeks after Sea Cloud shouted at me to do something
about my stinky armpits, Mother sent me to Shanghai for the
operation. Waipo had arranged everything. She had a distant
cousin who was the colleague of a doctor in Shanghai People's
Hospital whom she persuaded to do the operation. All cosmetic
surgeries were forbidden during the Cultural Revolution, since
making people look better through artificial methods belonged
to the bourgeois aesthetic value system. When Waipo found
him, he was cleaning the hospital bathrooms every day to redeem himself from his shameful past. I still don't understand
how she managed to convince him to take that risk.

"How is it?" Waipo would ask, pointing at her armpit with a
mysterious, slightly anxious look on her face. "No more smell,
eh?" This was always her first question, no matter how long we
hadn't seen each other. "You're lucky. Doctor Shi was the best
cosmetic surgeon in Shanghai. He said no to me at least five

times, so resolute. But I went to see him every day, in his home. I washed and cooked for him, and cleaned his place for two months. Finally he told me to take you to the hospital. I bowed to him. 'You've saved my granddaughter,' I said. 'Now she can live like a normal person.'"

Waipo paused here, as usual, as if to wait for my response. I never said anything, not because I was ungrateful to my grandma. After the operation, I did feel much better. I no longer walked around pressing my arms against my sides and bending my head. But I dared not wear short sleeves in summer or lift my arms in public baths. I still had to hide. Waipo's account touched me, but I didn't know what to say to her.

"Well, I still wonder why I did it for you," Waipo continued, obviously disappointed at my silence. "Your uncle is still mad at me. He blames his four failed operations on me. In a way, he's right. I ought to have begged Doctor Shi to help my only son first."

I saw my uncle Dong's armpits while he was weightlifting. They resembled smashed beehives. Scars upon scars, the rows of bad stitches, with a few trembling hairs. After all these torments, he still smelled like a rotten egg.

"But I have no regret. You needed it more than your uncle. Boys can get away with it more easily than girls. Doctor Shi is a good man. He risked his life for you, but when I sent him a basket of eggs, he refused to take them. He just said to me, 'I've taken care of your granddaughter. She'll be fine. She's a good girl.' I left the basket at his door. All those fresh eggs. Your mother told me to keep some for myself, but I didn't."

What was that *it?* I wished Waipo would call a spade a spade and just say *fox smell* instead of using *it* all the time. Her evasiveness only stimulated people's imagination and made them think I had some unspeakable disease. But if she had really used *hu chou,* could I have taken it? If I were not ashamed of it myself, I wouldn't have hidden my scars so diligently. I stretched my back and faked a yawn to stop my grandma's endless chatter. I'd heard the story at least twenty times. Waipo didn't buy those eggs. They were from the hens I raised. I never tasted the eggs either, although I had done all the dirty work. I was wearing a shirt with loose sleeves. The sleeves fell to my shoulders as I raised my arms to yawn. Waipo caught my hands, pulled down the sleeves and patted my shoulders as if to seal them in place.

"You're the lucky one, the lucky one. The scars hardly show," she murmured as she left the room to cook lunch.

In New York, I no longer need to hide the scars. From the silly questions my American friends asked, I realized they didn't even know about "cutting off the fox smell," a cosmetic operation that probably existed only in China. When they asked me whether I got the scars from huge pimples or eczema or child abuse, I just said "hmm" from my nose, or "I was too young to remember." Gradually the sleeves for my summer dresses became shorter and shorter until I only wore sleeveless shirts or sundresses with thin straps to show off my shoulders and arms. In the subway, I hold onto the strap to support myself, exposing my armpits without shame. No one bothers to look up, not the New Yorkers. Most of them doze off in their seats, withered from a day's work or the summer heat. Their curiosity has been worn out by too much stimulation. So many bizarre things in New York that take place right in your face, as frequent as the homeless walking through the trains asking for money, one after another, nonstop. You have no choice but to close your eyes, pretending to sleep. Only the tourists are still curious, looking around wide-eyed. They haven't learned to protect themselves.

Within two years of living in New York, I had had relationships with four men—one Chinese American, one Japanese-Irish hybrid, one Canadian Jew, and one mixture of Puerto Rican, African American, Chinese, Mexican, Portuguese. I broke up with them all, and broke their hearts, without the slightest hesitation or guilt, quite unlike the way I acted in China, where I had kept secret a relationship with a married man for five years. He finally went back to his wife and children, and the only concern I had for a long time was what I could do to ease his pain. But now I could end an intense relationship by leaving a message on the answering machine: "It's over and I no longer care to see you again."

When I broke up with the fourth man, I remembered Jian Ning's prophecy: "You're a fox spirit." No, I screamed to myself, I was no fox spirit. I just had no luck with men. My first lover lied to me about his two marriages and two kids (he was still married to his second wife although he wouldn't admit it). The second one was unbelievably stingy—he worked for some big company and could get reimbursed for his restaurant bills, of which I paid half; that is, he made money by "taking me out" (to quote his words), although he had tons of money in the bank. The third one was impotent, and the fourth one tried to blame me for the blisters on his penis. What else could I do but break up with them? I had to protect myself, being alone in a foreign country. If I were a fox spirit, I wouldn't have dropped them. I would have sucked them dry, at least of their money, if not their blood. I was no fox spirit, although I had fox smell scars on my armpits. Fox spirits never ended well. Concubine Yang was blamed for the fall of the country and was forced to hang herself by her emperor husband. Da Ji, the favorite concubine of King of Zhou, who turned herself into a beautiful woman from a fox to seduce Zhou and destroy the Shang Dynasty (16th–11th BC), was eventually beheaded. It was said that she would smile only when she saw people being tortured and screaming in pain. So the emperor invented different ways of torment to make her laugh. One of them was to make prisoners walk barefoot on a greasy bronze post suspended over a bed of fire.

I was thirty-three when I met John, an Italian American from Buffalo. He and his younger brother Bruno dressed, walked, and talked exactly like those machos from the western movies. It was hilarious. But John showed real respect for my scars. He was curious, but he wasn't nosy about them, didn't ask stupid questions. He just kissed them gently and told me, in a whisper, that they looked like flowers. It made me weep—the first time I had cried in front of another human being since I arrived in New York. I fell madly and shamelessly in love with him. One evening, after a simple dinner I bought and prepared—fried bean curd and Chinese broccoli with oyster sauce—we sat on the porch chatting and drinking the wine John had just brought back from Buffalo. John imitated the host of a TV talk show and made us all laugh and stamp our feet like lunatics. Suddenly he became gloomy. "My grandma is crazy," he said. "When we were having dinner, she pointed at me with her knife and asked me what was the matter. All my brothers had nice girlfriends. Why was I alone? She always believed I was the most promising boy. Now she thinks I should find a sugar mama, with lots of connections and money so that I can make as many movies as I want. Can you believe it?"

It was a hot July day, but I shivered in sweat. I curled my body, wishing it would just disappear in the chair. I was thirteen years older than John, almost old enough to be his mother, his sugar mama. But I was a poor alien. I could only afford to buy bean curd and broccoli for his dinner. The phone broke the silence. John dashed inside the house like a chased rabbit. From the porch, his voice and laughter sounded unnaturally loud. Bruno and I avoided looking at each other, not knowing how to start a new subject.

"Bruno, Sharon wants to speak to you," John shouted.

He returned to the porch, a huge leer on his face. "Oh God, oh my God," he moaned and laughed as he sank into the squeaking vine chair. "Poor Bruno, my poor Bruno."

"What's the matter?"

"Sharon wants to have coffee with him."

"What's wrong with that?"

"You've never met Sharon. She's the most repressed British woman during the day, but at night, with the help of some liquor, she's transformed into a female fox."

"What do mean by 'female fox'? Please explain," I shouted, but my voice was just a squeaky, hissing sound.

"You've never heard of that? A female fox is a kind of nymphomaniac, sucking men's energy through sex. I know that old Sharon. After a few drinks, she'll fuck anything with fur on it—dogs, cats, mice. Poor Bruno, he'll need ginseng. Do you have any of that stuff left? It will give him power so he can fuck her till she begs him to stop. Ha! ha! ha! . . ."

John laughed silently, shaking his head and hitting his thighs with his fists. To my horror, I suddenly noticed how much John looked like a fox in his grimace, with his small, sharp, white teeth and his uneven beard that stood up on his square jaw. Was there such a thing as a male fox spirit? I suddenly remembered a story from Pu Song Ling's *Liaozhai zhiyi* about how to vanquish a female fox spirit:

> A man was bewitched by a fox spirit. He moved to different places to get rid of her, but she followed him everywhere. A Taoist taught him the art of the bed-chamber and gave him some medicine that would

keep him erect as long as he wanted. At night, the fox
came as usual. He fucked her with tremendous power
and brutality. Soon the fox screamed in pain and
begged him to stop, but he plunged even harder until
her wailing subsided and her body no longer moved.
He looked and found her dead in his bed. He had
killed the fox spirit with his cock.

Time to run again, I said to myself.

That night, when John kissed my scars and murmured how
much they looked like flowers, the details of the operation
came back to me. With my eyes closed, I whispered the story to
John.

My youngest aunt took me to the hospital. She walked
quickly ahead of me, pulling my hand hard as if to prevent me
from escaping a slaughterhouse. The hallway was packed with
patients, all looking desperate and insane. The walls they
leaned on were covered with revolutionary slogans: DOWN WITH
REACTIONARY MEDICAL AUTHORITIES! CARRY THE PROLETARIAN
DICTATORSHIP TO THE END! The characters, twice as big as
human bodies, dwarfed the patients. I had to run to keep up
with my aunt. She was seven years older than me, very quick-
tempered. Before leaving, she had a terrible fight with Waipo.
She hated hospitals, hated having to take me there. People
would think she had to be operated on for the fox smell. Why
did she have to do the dirty work? But as usual, she always did
what she was told, after much whining and shouting.

We entered the operating room at the end of the hallway. An
old man with a medical mask was waiting for us. He didn't say
anything, but gestured to his nurse to help me take off my shirt
and lie down on the cot in the middle of the room. The nurse
lifted my arms above my head and began to shave my armpits.

Her gentle and caring touch relaxed me. The doctor filled a vial with transparent liquid from a bottle and came over to give me the injection. When he bent over, I saw his eyebrows raised in shock.

"How old are you?"

I hesitated for a moment. Before I left for the hospital, Waipo had warned me that I must tell the hospital personnel I was twenty-three. Doctors were reluctant to operate on younger people because the sweat glands might grow back and produce the odor again. But no one would have believed I was twenty-three. At fourteen, I looked nine or ten at the most, both in my face and my body.

"I'm going to be eighteen in two weeks, Doctor Shi."

He raised his eyebrows again in disbelief, but went on with the injections. Soon I felt him cutting and flaking the skin in my left armpit. My arm jerked up and down like a puppet as he pulled hard, but I didn't feel any pain. After he stitched the wound, he started to work on the other armpit.

When my aunt helped me dress, Doctor Shi gave her a bottle of pills. "For the pain," he explained. "Tonight will be the worst. But she can handle it. She's brave."

I could see his smile behind his mask. I wanted to wave goodbye to him, but my arms were in slings, so I just nodded and smiled before I left.

That is how I got scars like maple leaves on each of my armpits.

When I returned to China for my father's funeral, I spent two days in Shanghai. Waipo insisted on it, saying she might never be able to see me again, since she was seventy-one years old. For her age, she still had an incredible memory and endless energy. Every day she would talk about Doctor Shi until I could no longer take it.

"I don't get it, Waipo, why did you go to so much trouble for me that time? I wasn't even your favorite granddaughter."

Waipo looked hurt. "Nonsense. I love each of you equally." Seeing the expression on my face, she said quickly, "Give me some credit for that at least. If not for the operation, you would probably be living a different life. You should thank your mother too. She begged me to help you and paid for everything."

"But why me? Why didn't you have the operation? Why didn't mother? Why didn't my sisters?"

Waipo said nothing for a while. Very unusual of her. She always had a quick answer for everything. "Well, Seaweed," she finally opened her mouth, "to tell you the truth, we're different. Your mother and sisters are lucky people. They don't have fox smell. I have it, inherited from my grandma, and gave it to you. In that sense, you and I are ill-fated. But mine was never that bad. The smell was weak, easily covered with perfume and powder. Now I'm old. It no longer bothers me. You were different. At fourteen, it was already really bad and would only get worse as you grew older. I don't know whether it was your stubbornness and bad temper that made your odor so strong or whether the odor made you bad tempered. Anyway, both your mom and I agreed that the operation would be good for you. It might even change your personality. You were such a strange little girl, you know."

"I'm still the same, Waipo."

"Listen, Seaweed." Waipo suddenly looked anxious. "When you choose a husband, look into his ears first. If the inside is oily, don't even consider going out with him."

"What are you talking about, Waipo?" I laughed.

"Ninety percent of the people with oily ears have fox smell, just like you. If you marry such a person, your children are bound to inherit the odor. But if your husband is clean, half your kids will be spared. So choose a dry-eared man. Promise me?"

I kept laughing. My grandma wouldn't give up. I was already thirty-six (thirty-eight according to the Chinese custom of counting one's age), and she still wanted me to get married and have children. I wanted to tell her that my children, if I would ever have any, would never have to worry about the fox smell. In America, there were hundreds of kinds of deodorants to kill the odor. The most common brands were Secret, Right Guard, Dry Idea, Tickle, Lady's Choice, Teen Spirit, Shower to Shower, Speed, Power, and Ban.

CHU
JIA

⌒ Three weeks after I settled down in a Malaysian Chinese tailor's boardinghouse in Bay Ridge, a letter arrived from Waipo, forwarded from my sponsor's house in Flushing.

Granddaughter Seaweed,
  I'm so glad you've found such a beautiful, spacious room, all to yourself, and a job within such a short time. How much money are you making a month? What a lucky girl you are! I knew, ever since you were a kid, that the farther you got from home, the more successful you'd be. See, my prophecy has come true. First, you went to Hangzhou, then to Shanghai, now you're in New York. Everyone envies you. You won't forget your old *waipo*, who never leaves her messy room like an old turtle never leaves its pond? I need you to do me a favor. Keep your eye open for a suitable man for your *dayi*. No "barbarian," only Chinese, well-educated, healthy, good-looking, and well-off. Remember, your *dayi* is still a virgin, so don't give me a widower with two or three kids. Don't think that your *waipo* is trying to be fashionable like everyone else

because she asks you to look for a man in America. The truth is that the best Chinese men are all abroad. I know it's funny that a niece has to hunt a husband for her aunt. But I'm already *shan qiong shui jin*—at the end of my wits. Your *dayi* is forty-two. No matter how successful her career is, how much money she's making, she has to *chu jia,* right? A husband is a woman's final home to return to.

Holding the letter in my hand, I didn't know whether I should laugh or cry. Dayi was Waipo's second child, my first aunt. The relation between them always confused me. Waipo seemed to care for Dayi the most: she got up at five in the morning to prepare breakfast for Dayi, cooked her dinner and washed all her dirty clothing, even her underwear, with great pleasure and devotion. You would understand why it was a big deal if you heard how loudly and viciously she cursed my grandpa whenever she did his laundry or served him meals. Waipo devoted all her time and energy hunting for a perfect son-in-law. And believe me, Waipo had the energy of a super-woman, a memory with the capacity of the most advanced computer, the intelligence and cunning of the KGB. Every time she found a possible candidate for her daughter, she'd make a thorough investigation about the man's economic, political, and physical conditions, as well as his family background. She'd visit his workplace, talk to his boss and colleagues, even follow him to his home. Only when she was completely satisfied with the candidate would Waipo present his photo to Dayi and make her choose a date to meet the guy.

Dayi seemed to be completely devoted to her mother. On the first day of the month, she'd hand Waipo her salary, every fen of it, and Waipo would take it with both hands, count it twice, then draw out three five-yuan notes for Dayi—one for her monthly bus fare, one for her lunches, and one for her pocket money. This monthly ritual, carried out with great solemnity and piousness, had started when Dayi received her first pay at the age of twenty, and lasted for fifteen years till Dayi declared, on her thirty-fifth birthday, that she'd give Waipo twenty yuan a month and save the rest of her salary for her retirement since she had no husband or child to take care of her in her old age. She let Waipo choose her clothing, her food, and she met every candidate Waipo picked out for her. And Waipo consulted Dayi instead of her husband when she needed to make important decisions about things like letting her other daughters go to the countryside as educated youth, dealing with policemen, purchasing a television. When they bent their heads together under the dim lamp, discussing the family business in whispers, their shadows completely covered Waigong, my good-natured grandfather, who sat in his favorite chair in the corner, reading *Sun Zi Bin Fa*—a book on the art of war.

But the two did fight, and they fought fiercely over one subject—Dayi's marriage. Dayi went on every date Waipo fixed for her, but she rarely saw the same man twice. On the other hand, although Waipo looked vehemently for a suitable man for her daughter, when Dayi really started seeing one of the men she'd picked out, Waipo would immediately use all her investigative talents to find out the man's shortcomings, presenting them one after another to wake up Dayi—to use Waipo's own phrase, polish her eyes. For this tug-of-war, the strengths at each end of the rope were quite well matched: Waipo had her superhuman energy, KGB spying methods, and thundering noises; Dayi had her quiet, persistent obstinacy and a will of steel.

Of the five children, Dayi was Waipo's greatest pride. She was beautiful and elegant, with her smooth ivory skin, her soft pitch-black hair, and her long slender neck and fingers. The neighbors nicknamed her Swan. Anyone who saw her for the first time would stop breathing for a few seconds, then utter an exclamation or sigh mixed with admiration and envy. My mother was considered a beauty on the island. But when the two sisters got together, my mother looked like a country bumpkin: her skin was too dark and coarse, her features less refined, her voice too loud, and her gestures too exaggerated. I think that was why Mother preferred her other sisters to Dayi. My father, who loved my mother very much, and who was considered a *zhen ren jun zi*—a man of honor—hid a photo of Dayi in a volume of Mao's collected works, which my mother would be sure to never open. He was as enthusiastic—in my mother's words, hot-hearted—as Waipo about finding a husband for his sister-in-law. Every time his ship anchored in Shanghai, he'd rush to Waipo's third-floor apartment with a picture of some new bachelor Navy officer. I often caught him stealing glances at Dayi's neck and breasts, outlined sensually by the tight wool sweaters she often wore. Although my mother had four children, her breasts were not even half the size of Dayi's. I once overheard Mother tell Waipo that Dayi was probably not a virgin anymore. Her breasts couldn't have gotten that big unless they had been fondled by many men.

Not only was Dayi beautiful, but she was also smart. She was the only college graduate of her siblings. She had been promoted from a technician to a chief engineer, until finally she was appointed head of the technical department in Shanghai Machine Repair Factory. She also sang and danced well. On Sundays, if she had no dates, she'd take out three gigantic photo albums and tell me stories about each picture she'd taken at one of her performances, concerts, picnics, or graduation ceremonies. It was these photos that had made me decide that I'd go to college too, like Dayi.

"Ah Nue is like me in everything, her intelligence, her looks, only she was born in better years and luckier than me," Waipo often said. In terms of intelligence, she wasn't exaggerating. Without any school education, Waipo had somehow taught herself to read letters and newspapers. At the beginning of the Cultural Revolution, everyone was forced to memorize *lao san pian*—Mao's three long articles, "Serve the People," "In Memory of Norman Bethume," and "The Foolish Man Moves the Mountain." I could never do it, no matter how many times I was punished to stand in the corner or stay after school, whereas Waipo learned them by heart just by listening to my practice. She could remember all her children's and friends' telephone numbers and the dates of important occasions without the slightest hesitation. Dayi often said, half as a joke and half with helpless bitterness, that her mother should become the head of the Intelligence Department.

As for looks, any comparison was wishful thinking on Waipo's part. Except for her skin, Dayi inherited her fine looks from her father—his high cheekbones and straight nose as well as his tall, well-proportioned figure. I often watched him sitting quietly in his chair and wondered why my grandfather, so handsome and gentlemanly, so well positioned as an accountant in an important Hong Kong Bank in the 1940s, had married Waipo, who was only a factory girl at the time.

Ah Nue wasn't Dayi's real name, but a colloquial term for girls. Waipo often called me *xiao nue*—little girl—when she was very pleased or angry with me. She'd sworn, when Dayi handed over her first salary, that she'd find the best man for her daughter, that she'd never let Ah Nue repeat her own tragedy in marriage. Waipo couldn't stand being under the same roof with her husband for more than half an hour. Hardly five minutes would pass without Waipo picking on him: he ate like a pig, sat like a woman in labor, or stood in the middle of the room like a dumb wire post. If he was quiet, she'd scream at him for being like a dead log. But when he answered her, she'd make a big commotion, slapping herself on the face, beating her own chest and thighs, and calling him the villain who had ruined her life. She had many names for her husband. Her favorite ones were "dead old head," and "old turtle egg."

But fair is fair, Waipo had never neglected her job of taking care of her husband. She always made sure he was neatly dressed, well fed, and put to bed comfortably. Once Waigong had pneumonia. Waipo stayed up three days and nights in the hospital, changing his ice bags, wiping his sweat, bringing him water. She kept murmuring, "Don't abandon us, Old Head, I won't let you go before me." During those days, she dropped the word *dead* from the names she called Waigong, but as soon as he returned home, she started calling him "dead turtle egg" again.

I asked her one day, after Waigong had just fled from her vicious curses, why she treated her husband like an enemy. She gave me a sad look, and said, "Xiao Nue, if you knew what he did to me in the past, you'd probably kill him." Then she understood that I was questioning her contradictory behavior toward her husband and sighed. "Xiao Nue, he's still the *zhu xin gu*, the backbone, the pillar of our family, no matter how bad and useless. It really doesn't matter whether he functions as a backbone or not, but as long as he's here, we're safe." Seeing that I was even more puzzled, she pointed at Mao's portrait on the wall. "You see, we all know that Chairman Mao is too sick and old to make any decisions, but we still wish him *wan shou wu jiang*—long life—every morning. Why? Because if he's gone, the country will go up in flames."

Waipo loved money, so her definition for the best man at that time was a rich man, the son of a capitalist who would inherit money and a handsome garden house from his father. But the Cultural Revolution upset her plan: all the capitalists and their descendants were driven off their property and became the class enemies of society. So rich men were out of the question. And the intellectuals and cadres had been forced to step aside from their positions, being "swept into the garbage can of history," to use another fashionable phrase. The only possible candidates were Army officers and Red Guards, actually officers only, because Waipo had never liked those emotional, violent, and revolutionary teenage Red Guards. During the years when the Army was popular, Father, who brought one or two pictures of his colleagues to Waipo on each visit to Shanghai, was received with extreme hospitality, although Waipo never stopped referring to him as "country bumpkin," "northern barbarian," or "garlic head" behind his and my mother's backs.

After the Army's popularity faded, Waipo's attention turned to *gong xuan dui*—the team of factory workers for the propaganda of Mao's thoughts. They had taken over the country's universities and schools. We called it "workers step onto the stage of history." When that was over, Waipo became crazy about doctors. They were among the first intellectuals to be liberated from cow sheds and allowed to practice—to serve the people. There was a great demand for them; patients had to stand in line from four o'clock in the morning in order to see a doctor in the afternoon. Those who needed to be hospitalized often had to wait for months for a bed in a hospital. Apart from that, doctors could also write sick leave notes for their patients (whether they were ill or not) and prescribe free medicines (some were actually tonics). Their offices were often stuffed with fresh eggs, ham, chickens, fish, dried fruits, and other rationed goods that patients used as bribes—we called it "walking through the back door"—in order to be on the visiting lists.

Thus Waipo adjusted her standards promptly and diligently. I said diligently because things changed more and more rapidly toward the end of the Cultural Revolution, and many different people had "stepped onto the stage of history" and then been "thrown into the garbage can of history," and I'd witnessed many different "best candidates" climbing three floors to enter Waipo's room, then leaving in failure. Neighbors gave Dayi another nickname: *zou ma deng,* which is a lantern with cut-paper figures that revolve when it is lit, something like a dizzying merry-go-round. However, no matter how open-minded, how fashionable Waipo was, I could tell that her strongest wish was to get a doctor for her son-in-law, because a doctor belonged to the category of intellectuals and had a prospect of making a lot of money or goods, and Waipo herself could always get free treatment and medicines. So when she found Doctor Lee, she really pushed hard to make Dayi submit to her wish. That was the first time I witnessed the war between them.

It was Dayi's twenty-eighth birthday. That morning, Waipo had made Waigong get up at three o'clock to buy fish, shrimp, pork, eggs, and vegetables at the market, and she had prepared eight dishes for dinner. I'd never seen her so cheerful and good tempered during my visit that summer. She didn't curse anybody, didn't even scold me when I broke her favorite bowl. Dayi didn't return home as she'd promised. At nine-thirty, Waipo woke me up at the table and put a bowl of rice with two shrimp, a chunk of pork, and some vegetables into my hand. I glanced at the eight covered dishes. Waipo was picking out the two fattest chunks of pork and pressing them into Waigong's rice bowl, which was covered with four shrimp and vegetables. Waipo didn't serve herself. She was determined to wait for Dayi. I gulped my share, hoping that Waipo would give me some fish. But I knew she wouldn't because she was saving the whole fish for Dayi's birthday. After all, Dayi made the highest salary in the family, and Waigong, though he made less, was the only other wage earner and the backbone of the family. If he got to eat two chunks of pork and four shrimps, it was only fair, especially since Waipo always ate the leftovers herself.

I finished my supper quickly and spread out a mattress under the dinner table. It was my own choice to sleep there because it was so much cooler to lie on the floor in the summer than on the bed. Besides, I loved to have the whole mattress to myself. Under the square table, surrounded by the thick table legs, it was almost like having a room of my own. Not that I didn't like sharing a bed with my sister and Dayi, or with my grandma and grandpa—I'd been begging my parents to spend a summer with them in this messy but warm one-room apartment. To tell the truth, I felt much more at home here than in my parents' place. For the first twelve years of my life, I always shared a bed with someone. By the time my mother had her fourth child, Sea Gull, our bed had to hold four sleepers: Nainai, Sea Tiger, Sea Cloud, and me. Sea Gull slept in her crib for a year, then in my parents' bed for a year before she was sent to Shanghai. If there had been any extra room in our queen-sized bed, my mother would have put Sea Gull there too. Often in my dreams, my brother's foot on my belly became a bomb someone had planted in my stomach, my sister's arm became a snake choking my neck, and the smell of Nainai's bound feet made me dream of falling into a latrine pit. The mere thought of human flesh pressing against my sides, even if it was the flesh of my siblings and Nainai, would make me want to throw up. For the last two years, I'd been sobbing before going to bed and waking up lying on the cement floor in the morning. My mother always said I had oversensitive nerves and that I was prone to allergy because I'd been spoilt as a first-born. But she was finally alarmed enough at my strange behavior that she sent me to Shanghai for a vacation.

I was awakened by Dayi's sobbing and Waipo's angry voice. "What do you mean you don't like him? He's the most popular doctor in the best hospital in Shanghai. I've talked to his bosses and colleagues. He's the only son. Think of his parents' two-bedroom apartment that you'll inherit in the future. So what if he still lives with them? Who doesn't live with their parents? Besides, he's so good-looking. Ah Nue, you have no reason to reject him."

"Mama, are you choosing a person or a commodity for me?"

The silence made me open my eyes. I saw Waipo sitting on the edge of her bed beating on her chest with both fists as if she were choking. When she finally spoke, her voice trembled with repressed fury. "You're still waiting for him, eh, your first love. He's bewitched you with his honey talk, his flower dew. What do you see in him? He's so tiny, like a shrimp, twenty years older than you. So what if he's a professor at Beijing University. Don't forget he's an associate professor. What are you going to do when you're married? Live apart forever? You know that it's impossible for you to find a job in Beijing or for him to find a job in Shanghai. Also, do you know his family background? His father is a historical counterrevolutionary. And your flower-dew shrimp, thanks to his big mouth, has been a target for criticism in each political movement. Who knows when he'll be exiled to Qinhai Province, a place where even grass doesn't grow. Will you follow him there?"

"I will."

Waipo pulled her hair and swayed back and forth. She opened her mouth wide, but no sound came out. She didn't want to disturb Waigong sleeping soundly on the other side of the bed. Her face turned from red to purple, her arms and legs waved in the air fanatically like a drowning person. Her feet kicked up the sheet that hung over the bed, exposing Waipo's collections of dusty jars, bottles, trunks, old shoes, and newspapers. The two queen-sized beds—one for Waipo and Waigong and the other for Dayi and my sister—took up half of the room, and the space underneath the beds was used for storage. Extending from the foot of Dayi's bed was a tall, thin closet, four trunks piled on top of each other to the ceiling, and a food cabinet on top of another cabinet for bowls and dishes. The table I was lying beneath stood in the middle of the room against a huge bookcase in which Waigong kept his books. Every time he needed to get a book, Waipo would curse at the top of her lungs as she helped him move the table and afterward, dusted the shelves. Against the window were a desk and a sofa chair. The chamber pot was hidden in the curtained corner next to Waipo's bed. Not an inch of room space was wasted.

Waipo was finally able to cry out. "My daughter, my own daughter, is trying to kill me. Old heaven, what have I done to you to make me suffer like this? You made me a tiger, why did you send me a dragon daughter to battle me? Such a miserable life, not a single day of happiness since I was married."

"If you hate marriage so much, Mama, why are you forcing me into that trap? If you are so miserable with Dad, don't you think you should learn your lesson and let me find the man I love? That Doctor Lee of yours, he's creepy behind his creamy looks. He's the one who has flower dew, and you're the one who's bewitched. Not me."

"Ah Nue, you know that a girl can't live with her parents forever. An old maid gets a bad reputation. Our neighbors have already started calling you bad names. Besides, where can you go when your dad and I are gone? Who will take care of you?"

"I can take care of myself. I'm twenty-eight years old. If I can supervise five hundred people in my department, I'm sure I can wash my own clothing and cook my own dinner. I'm not going anywhere, Mama. This is my home. For eight years, since I started working, I've been contributing all I have to keep things going. I have a stake here."

"Have you lost your mind? You know your brother will take over this room once we're gone. You don't have the right to claim it."

Under the table, Dayi's hands grasped her knees to stop them from shaking, but her toes wriggled violently within the black cotton shoes Waipo had made. "How enlightening!" Her tone was sarcastic now. "All these years, what you've been telling me—that I'm a hundred times better than a son—is just flower dew then. Yes, I'm a hundred times better than my brother in terms of giving you money. At least, you don't have to worry about my stealing from you like my brother does. By the way, Mother, since I'm just a no-right-to-claim daughter, I guess I have no right to contribute my salary to this household. And you, Mother, have no right to interfere with whom I love and marry."

With trembling hands, Waipo groped under her pillowcase and took out a letter. She threw it on the table. "Read it. Read the great news your faithful lover gives you. He's getting married, while you're still waiting for him like a fool. I took the trouble to keep this letter so that it wouldn't break your heart. But do you have any feelings for me?"

"How dare you? How dare you open my mail and hide it from me? I hate you. I'll never forgive you."

"Ah Nue, don't talk like this. I was just trying to help you."

"Don't you ever call me *ah nue* again! My name is Shen Yuan!" Dayi shrieked.

Waigong's voice came from the corner of the bed, loud and stern, unlike his usual amiable tone. "Old woman, you're going too far this time. Leave Yuan alone."

Waipo jumped to her feet, looked at her husband in disbelief, then turned to Dayi for support. Standing between the table and bed, she opened and closed her mouth like a fish gasping for air. When she finally understood that her husband was addressing her, she groaned and rushed out of the room. From the terrace came her wailing, mixed with rhymed words and melody. After listening for a while, I realized Waipo was telling her life story: She'd lost her mother at seven, was sold to a neighboring village as a child bride, ran away from the maltreatment of her mother-in-law when she was twelve, and sold herself to a textile factory in Shanghai as an indentured laborer. For five years, she worked without holidays or salary. When her contract was over, she thought she could have a better life with her skills and intelligence. But fate blinded her eyes and let her be seduced by a lazy, heartless man. She had five children, one after another, and spent her days and nights washing and mending smelly socks, while the good-for-nothing man brought "pheasants"—whores—home. She tolerated it all, thinking her children would compensate for her suffering. But they all betrayed her. What an ill-fated woman she was!

I sobbed under the table. It was heartbreaking to hear Waipo's story. I loved Waigong as much as Waipo. He knew so many things although he hardly ever opened his mouth, and he was gentle and kind. I glanced at Waigong. He'd covered himself completely with a blanket. Dayi was sitting on the bed reading the letter, her lips and hands trembling. Suddenly she stood up, moved a chair to the pile of trunks and fetched a small leather case from the top. She unlocked it on the floor. Inside were letters neatly lined and piled. She opened one envelope. Before she started reading, she was already choking with sobs. Meanwhile, Waipo's wailing became louder, but no one paid any attention to her. Lying under the table, I felt paralyzed.

Dayi took the iron dust bin from behind the door, poured the letters into it and lit a match. Watching the flames rise in the dust bin, I could no longer control my tears. Don't be sad, Dayi, I cried in my heart. You won't be lonely in your old age. I'll be your daughter. I'll take care of you. I'll have a beautiful apartment, just for you and me.

I crawled out and walked to Dayi. Before I opened my mouth, Dayi said sternly, "Go back to sleep, Seaweed. A *xiao nue* shouldn't overhear big people's conversation. Go now, or I'll not take you out to movies anymore."

The next few days were followed by a cold war. Waigong slept in his office to avoid Waipo's fury. I hardly saw Dayi either, because I would already be asleep when she came home at midnight. Out of boredom and curiosity, I looked up the word *nue* which had made Dayi furious that night. There was no such word in my dictionary for elementary students. I took out Waigong's big dictionary. It wasn't there either. I stayed up late that night to ask Dayi. She was chewing, with much difficulty, the cold and hard soy beans from the day before, having pushed aside the fresh dishes her mother had laid in front of her. She advised me to look for it under the standard pronunciation *nan*, as *nue* was only used in Shanghai dialect. I still couldn't find it. "How strange, how strange!" Dayi murmured. "I've heard this word all my life, but it's not even in a dictionary."

I asked Dayi if she knew how to write it. She frowned as she tried to remember. "I'm sure I've seen it somewhere. Try this. You know how to write the word *prisoner*, right? It's composed of two parts: four walls and person. Okay, keep the basic component 'four walls,' and fill in with the character 'girl.'" She suddenly stopped, her face twisted in pain as if the hard soy beans had broken her tooth. Waipo rushed to her with a hot towel. Dayi took it silently, a sign for reconciliation, and wiped her face slowly. When she finished, she turned to me. "Seaweed, sometimes it's better not to know everything. Go to bed, now. Tomorrow is Sunday. I'll take you and your sister to the Nanjing Road."

That was sixteen years ago, 1969. Even if I hadn't been an ignorant, twelve-year-old country bumpkin, I still couldn't have figured out why, out of so many other Chinese characters with the component "four walls," Dayi had picked "prisoner." She could have used *guo* (country), or *gu* (solid), or *hui* (come back). Anyway, since we found out how the character was formed, it had never been uttered again. Not even Waipo, who had used it the most.

Another glance at Waipo's letter: I turned my attention to the awkward, childish handwriting. It must be the work of my cousin, daughter of my third aunt. Waipo couldn't write herself, so she bribed her grandchildren to write the kinds of letters her own children or husband refused to do, like letters urging her relatives or friends to introduce men to Dayi, or letters to investigate Dayi's boyfriend's background. For each letter, I had received five fen. How much would she give my cousin now? The little girl wrote the character *jia*—a woman getting married—incorrectly. It should have two parts: girl and home. My cousin had left out the left component "girl," and turned the meaning of the phrase—a girl getting married—into *chu jia*— becoming a nun or a monk.

I was shocked by this discovery. The mistake was quite unforgivable for a sixth-grade student. Was it just a slip of the hand? Had the girl, like me, after witnessing the ugly battles between Dayi and Waipo, developed a phobia for marriage? *Chu jia*, the same sounds had two meanings. Were they really that different? To become a nun, one had to annihilate all her emotions and desires. When a girl got married, the only advice her mother gave her was to forget about her former comforts and habits in order to devote her heart and soul to serving her husband.

I opened my biggest dictionary to pinpoint the origin of *jia*. Nothing enlightening, except for the two terms in which *jia* was used as a transitive verb: *jia huo* and *jia yuan*—to marry (shift) the misfortune or hatred to someone else. Ask a Chinese man why women were associated with disasters, he'd immediately give you a list of the women who'd ruined kings and brought down empires. Even our great saint Confucius, known for his kindness and wisdom, complained that women and children were the hardest to raise.

Out of curiosity, I counted the words with the component of *nu*—woman. Of 223 words, many of them reflected the concept that women were the source of all misfortunes and therefore must be hated and oppressed: *yao* (beautiful, evil, alien); *du* (jealousy); *nu* (slaves); *ru* (obey, follow). To commit adultery, to deceive one's husband was the most hated crime, and the word *jian* was formed of three women. It was not by accident that the word for a man getting married—*qu*—was made of two parts: fetch and woman, and that the latter was put underneath.

The only exception was *hao,* composed of two parts: woman and son, meaning "good." A woman was not a woman unless she bore a son to her husband and his family. So when my sister Sea Cloud was divorced after she gave birth to a daughter, she had only herself and her failed womb to blame.

My head started hurting from all these discoveries. I put the dictionary back into my suitcase, and Waipo's letter back into the envelope. Maybe Dayi was right: sometimes it's better not to know everything. As for her marriage, I really couldn't help much. It was a problem with a long history.

One day, out of the blue, I asked a new acquaintance, a scholar of ancient Chinese literature, what was the word for "women's marriage" that had appeared in the earliest literary works. He gave me a strange look and told me that it was *yu gui*, from *The Book of Songs*. When I asked again what it meant, he looked appalled by my ignorance. "A girl doesn't have a real home until she marries. That's why we say *yu gui*—return home—for a girl getting married." I nodded in gratitude. His information had explained my mother's strange letters recently. No matter how many photos of my apartment I'd sent her, she still asked me when I'd have my own home. In her last letter, she warned me that if I didn't marry this year, I wouldn't have another chance till I was fifty-five. The oracle was absolutely true because it came from the back of a five-hundred-year-old sacred turtle. It also dawned on me why a middle-aged Chinese woman poet had smiled meaningfully when I invited her to have dinner at my place, and said, patting me on my shoulder, "Why don't you wait till you have a home."

Two years passed by quickly. One day I received Waipo's letter announcing Dayi's marriage. The bridegroom, fifty years old, was also a virgin. He was an associate professor at Shanghai Institute of Sea Transportation, the first nephew of a deceased minister, and lived with his mother in a two-bedroom apartment in the suburbs. "Everything seems perfect, except he's so cheap," Waipo said bitterly. "Guess what he fed us at his wedding banquet? Bean curd soup! Outrageous! Your *dayi* will have lots of *ku tou*—bitter heads—to swallow in the future, I tell you. And you know what? He's not even good-looking. Every time I look at his puffy eyelids, sagging cheeks, and pot belly, I want to throw up all the bean curd soup I'd swallowed at the banquet back in his ugly face. Your poor *dayi*, all these years of picking and choosing have put her mind at sixes and sevens. At the age of forty-four, she fell into the hands of a guy with the face of a turtle."

AMERICAN
VISA

~ Sea Cloud asked me to help her get out of China on the night when we were sailing from Shanghai to Dinghai to attend Father's funeral. I was surprised as well as pleased. Sea Cloud was the most beautiful and sociable of the three sisters in our family. My parents used to ask me why I couldn't look and behave like Sea Cloud. When she was born, her long eyelashes, small and well-shaped lips, and soft black curls impressed all the nurses and doctors. My father looked out of the window and saw the rising sun dyeing the clouds into orange, purple, gray, and green. *"Haixia*—Sea Cloud, that's her name," he cried out. He liked it so much that he even changed my original name—Lena—to Seaweed. It matched my brownish skin color quite well. I often wondered whether my fate might have been different if Sea Cloud had never been born. As years passed by, I began to think that I was no longer jealous of her. I was the only person in my family who had earned an MA degree and was making U.S. dollars in New York. But as soon as I saw Sea Cloud, my heart twinged with jealousy again. I'd give up everything, even my green card, to have her eyes, her nose, her skin. When she brought me hot water to wash my face, and did my laundry—things my parents had made me do for her when we were young—I felt flattered and uneasy. I begged her to stop serving me like that and told her I would be happy to help her if she needed anything.

"Sister," she said, her dark velvet eyes filled with anxiety, "I want to go to America."

I couldn't say anything for a while. Sea Cloud had only a high school diploma, which she had received at the end of the Cultural Revolution—when students did nothing but torture their teachers, memorize Mao's red book, and work in the countryside and factories. She had worked only as a warehouse keeper for the past ten years and didn't have any particular skills. She would have to apply for a tourist visa from the U.S. Embassy. As far as I knew, the embassy issued very few tourist visas to Chinese. Even if she got it, what could she do in New York? She didn't speak any English except to shout "Long live Chairman Mao!" She wouldn't be able to find a job, not even a restaurant job. I looked at her long delicate hands and her slim waist. How could she possibly survive there? Of course she might attract some rich guy and get married. But was that what she wanted?

"Help me, Sister," Sea Cloud pleaded, and it hurt me more than anything. She had never begged from anybody like this. "I have no way out. I don't even have a place of my own."

Sea Cloud had just been divorced after four years of a disastrous marriage. After she gave birth to a baby girl, her husband started to go out to avoid his mother, who wanted a grandson to inherit the family name. He was the only son. But having another child was absolutely against government policy. He began to see other girls, leaving Sea Cloud at home to take the brunt of his mother's scorn. Sea Cloud couldn't turn to Mother for help because she had warned her about that man and his family. Finally, when her husband was absent from home week after week and began to treat her like a piece of garbage, she asked for a divorce. The husband didn't consent. In court Sea Cloud presented the love letters from his mistresses. She got the divorce but lost her child. Her husband had complete custody of the girl. She couldn't even see her daughter. After the divorce, she didn't even have a place to stay. Her ex-husband made sure she didn't get a dormitory in her factory where he was an assistant manager. He even continued taking her salary, saying she was still financially responsible for her daughter. Two months ago, Sea Gull found her a part-time job in Beijing, which solved her problem temporarily. But she still didn't have a home.

I knew what it was like to be homeless, with no one standing behind you. I should help Sea Cloud. But she had almost no chance of getting a visa, and I hated to give her an empty promise. With hesitation, I said, "I can sponsor you, but you have to wait till Sea Gull gets her visa, and you must promise me to learn some English."

Tears began to fill her eyes. She nodded and wiped her eyes with her fingertips. I turned away. I couldn't bear to see her cry. Was I too cruel to make her wait her turn and make her learn English? God knows when Sea Gull could get her visa!

About eight months ago, I had received a letter from Sea Gull just before going to Vermont for the summer. She begged me to rescue her from the police, who were investigating her activities in the Tiananmen Square event. She had taken photos of the students on a hunger strike. If she couldn't come to America by September, she was bound to be punished and sent to the most remote province.

"Please, Sister," she wrote, "enroll me in any school, any major, as long as I can get out fast. I'm really scared. I swear I won't be a burden to you. I'll do anything to support myself. If you don't believe me, this letter will be my affidavit. You can show it to me and remind me of my promise if I ever bother you."

The letter upset me terribly. When the students started their demonstrations and hunger strike at Tiananmen Square, I called Sea Gull and asked her if she had been to the square and if she would take some photos for me. In my excitement, I told her that she shouldn't miss the chance of participating in the greatest historical event of the 1990s. She hadn't been to the square yet because her dormitory was twenty miles away from the city and the bus service was terrible. The bank she worked for was a few blocks away from the square. But her bosses had warned her not to be involved and the bank had temporarily canceled their one-hour rest period after lunch to prevent the employees from sneaking out. But she promised she would go immediately. She wouldn't be in trouble now if I hadn't asked for the photos. I was responsible, but how could I possibly get her to New York as a student within one month? It was the end of July, too late to apply for the fall semester. Even if there was no deadline, how could she be accepted by a college, get the I-94 form from the school, apply for her passport from the police bureau, and then her visa from the U.S. Embassy within one month? Just the materials she had to gather for the application alone—her transcripts, recommendation letters, my bank statement, and an affidavit to declare that I would provide her with all the necessary tuition fees and living expenditures during her years of studying—would take more than one month. Usually the whole process, from filling out the application to obtaining a visa, takes one or two years—if you are lucky. Didn't she have any common sense? She seemed to have some because she didn't ask me to get her to America as a tourist.

What did she expect me to do? I didn't have any power or connections. I was only a first-grade teacher in a Chinatown public school working under a temporary labor certificate with a per diem substitute license.

I was irritated by the implication in her letter that I was cheap. Since I came to New York, I had been telling her to study English so that she could pass the TOEFL, an English language test required for non-English international students to study in American colleges. Sea Gull had a bachelor's degree in bank finance with an excellent background in math. To get a master's degree in accounting or computer science would be very easy for her, and the job market was also good. But she had never shown any interest in my suggestion until now. Besides she didn't have any idea what surviving in the U.S. was like when she swore she wouldn't use a penny of mine. If she came here, she would have to pay for her food, shelter, and transportation, which would cost at least $700 a month. When the semester began, she would have to pay $2,000 for her tuition. She didn't have any money, not even for the fare from Beijing to New York, which would cost almost her annual salary. What made her believe she could survive without my help?

She must have been desperate to say things like that. Still, it hurt my feelings when my sister thought so badly of me. I had no other choice but to help her. She was my sister and had a college education. She should have a chance. I called Queens, Baruch, and City colleges to send Sea Gull the application forms, and called my friend Jack to mail her a form from the Graduate Center of CUNY. He worked in the international students office there and could do it for free. Then I rushed to Citibank and paid forty-five dollars emergency service fee to get my bank statement on the same business day, went downtown to 26 Plaza to get an affidavit from the Immigration and Naturalization Service, notarized it, then went to the post office to

mail the documents. In the envelope I enclosed five checks—
one to the TOEFL Center in Princeton for the sum of $35, and
four blank checks for the colleges. She could fill in the necessary amount each college charged for the application. About
two hundred dollars were gone even before she had started the
application.

Everything went quite well. Sea Gull managed to mail all the
materials to the colleges in New York just before her bank sent
her to a small town on the coast of the South China Sea. If she
passed the English test, if one of the colleges accepted her, and
if the U.S. Embassy granted her a visa, we'd be able to meet in
New York the next fall. But the road to America was full of
mines. Anything could happen to ruin her chance.

Both my sisters desperately needed help, but my bank account
was large enough to sponsor only one person at a time. I had
put away three thousand dollars for Sea Gull's tuition and first
month's expenditures. My original plan was that once Sea Gull
settled down in New York, we could both help Sea Cloud to
come to America, if she wanted to. At that time Sea Cloud was
still living with her husband and her parents-in-law. I hadn't expected her situation would become so tumultuous. I quickly
went over all the friends who might be willing to sponsor her.
None came to my mind. Being a sponsor meant one had to sign
an affidavit that said he or she must support the beneficiary
financially for at least one year. Although it didn't mean anything, Americans didn't like to do it. Suddenly I felt furious
with myself and Mother. My sisters needed my help, and I was
lettting them down. But why should I be the only person to
solve their problems? Sea Cloud's husband and her mother-in-
law wouldn't have dared to treat her like this if Mother had
stood behind Sea Cloud. And the least thing Mother could do

was to offer shelter to her daughter. Her new apartment had two bedrooms. But she would rather keep it empty and watch Sea Cloud drift around homeless. What kind of mother was she?

"I don't understand why she won't help you," I said, staring at the rising moon from the sea as I leaned on the rail. "You've always been her favorite child. I used to be terribly jealous of you."

Her silence made me turn to her. In the moon light, I saw tears gathering in her eyes. "This is so strange, Sister," she finally said. "I've always been extremely jealous of *you*. How many nights I've cried in my blanket, wishing Mother would treat me—train me, I should say—as she trained you."

"You call it trai–, training?" I stuttered, half exasperated, half stunned by what I'd just heard. "All that beating, cursing, and insulting, all those back-breaking chores? Are you out of your mind? Or do you just not remember how you made me cry with the candies, cookies, and new clothing Mother gave you, you alone, and how I had to stay home cooking three meals a day for the entire family while you were out playing with your friends. You call that training? I just don't believe it!"

"You don't understand, Sister," Sea Cloud raised her voice to make me listen. "Mother really loves you, in her own way. She recognized how smart and strong-willed you were, even as a child. She believed that you could *gan dashi*—do big things—if you were trained properly. That's why she gave you so much work—to test your ability and make you tough. True, she never told you how great you were. That's because she thought praise would only spoil you. When you were not around, she never stopped telling us to learn from you. You know, sometimes I was so jealous that I wanted to knock you down with an ax. Mother loves you more than anyone else."

The wind blew, shredding the perfect reflection of the moon on the surface of the sea into thousands of pieces. I shook my head, then nodded. My brain was boiling inside my head. Sea Cloud's words had turned all my perceptions and judgments upside down. So Mother had loved me, and loved me more than anyone else! How come I never felt it? Perhaps we all remembered our past from a different point of view. Maybe perception was just a fraud.

"Look at yourself and look at me, Sister," Sea Cloud's voice seemed to emerge from the bottom of the sea. "How different our lives are! You have a master's degree from an American college, whereas I barely graduated from high school. You're so capable, and I'm so weak, always asking for help. I have nothing except for my looks. It has brought me nothing but bad luck. Besides, how long will it last? It's just like my name—Haixia— Sea Cloud, vanishing like the mist in the sea when the sun comes out. If only I had half of your intelligence and ability! I envy you, Sister, but I'm also proud of you and happy for your success!"

I put my arm around her shoulder, something I had never done in my life. She stopped talking, her head leaned on my shoulder. We watched the moon resume its perfect image again on the water. I had never felt so close to Sea Cloud. "You're a beautiful woman, both inside and outside," I murmured. "I've always wished that I had half of your beauty."

We looked at each other and laughed.

"Sister," she said, holding my shoulders with her hands, "help Sea Gull first. I can wait. I can keep working in Beijing. My colleagues are nice to me. One of them has even offered to take me to Hong Kong. Maybe I should go there first, then try to go to America. Maybe I can even get there before Sea Gull."

She paused, then added, "I'm ashamed to be so eager to leave the country. I hadn't even thought about it before the divorce.

I'm lazy and easy to please, not like you, always energetic, always looking for something. I guess my ex-husband really pushed me hard. But I don't understand why everyone else is so anxious to leave. Mother, Brother, Aunt, Uncle, and all my friends, all have good families, apartments, furniture, good jobs, but all they talk about is how to go abroad. I used to laugh at them. Now I'm one of them."

I couldn't answer her, being haunted by the same shame myself. At least my sisters had their excuses. What was mine? If I had stayed at Fudan, a most prestigious college in the southern China, I would have become an assistant professor, had a family and children. Now I was still single. My so-called career—*dashi*—was nothing but teaching forty hours a week in an elementary school, and I was always worried whether the Board of Education would hire me for the next semester. The apartment I shared with four strangers in Flushing swarmed with roaches. I had two big lumps in my shoulders from stress and the heavy dull pain drove me crazy day and night. Would Sea Cloud still think highly of me when she knew the truth? Why was I helping more people go abroad?

When I went back to New York, Sea Cloud's sad face haunted my dreams for weeks. Finally I went to the Immigration Department again and got two affidavits for tourists. I mailed them to my sisters along with two bank statements. Sea Cloud could try to apply for a tourist visa first. Sea Gull could also use it just in case she failed the test and couldn't be accepted by any college. I had done my best and whether they would succeed depended on their own luck.

Sea Gull wrote me immediately. The notarization on my affidavit was going to expire in June, just when she would start applying for her visa. Should she get a new affidavit or just change the month to September? It shouldn't be hard since it was in Arabic numerals. She also needed a letter to the police bureau and u.s. Embassy explaining that I was her sister and sponsor, and that I needed her badly in New York. "Please be polite and sweet in your letter," she wrote.

This was too much for me. If Sea Gull had stopped panicking and done some thinking, she would have noticed that the expiration date of the public notary had nothing to do with the validity of the affidavit. The notarization only proved that I was the person who signed the affidavit. I had to show my photo ID and sign the affadavit in front of the public notary. My name wouldn't expire along with the notarization. Besides, I would have to take a day off in order to go to the Immigration Department, stand in line for hours to get a form, notarize it, then stand in line again in the post office to register-mail it. I had used up all my sick days and business days, and I would have to take days off without pay. Besides, my principal wouldn't like it and I needed her good opinion of me to continue my contract. I told Sea Gull in my letter that she shouldn't worry about the affidavit, and that she mustn't change the date on it. I also told her to write the letters to the police and embassy herself and sign my name because I really didn't know how to do it.

I didn't hear from her again, nor from Sea Cloud. Sea Gull must be mad at me and Sea Cloud too proud to write. At Shanghai Airport, she had told me that she'd write only when she had accomplished something, like making a lot of money or going abroad on her own.

In June, my aunt called me from Shanghai and told me that Sea Cloud was about to leave for West Germany and Sea Gull had gotten a passport and was applying for a visa. She didn't know which country. Her mother had mentioned that Sea Cloud had a lot of connections and was trying to help Sea Gull go to Germany, too. But they were acting secret and hostile as if they were competing with each other. They wouldn't tell her anything. Not even Sea Gull, who grew up with my aunt till she was in high school. It hurt, she complained. My aunt had learned the news from her mother, with whom both Sea Cloud and Sea Gull were staying. She asked me if I knew anything about it and if I knew whether Sea Gull had passed her test and been accepted by any American college. She noticed that Sea Gull was very unhappy and nervous.

I felt betrayed when I put down the phone. Neither of my sisters had had the decency to tell me what was going on after what I had done for them. Sea Cloud might want to hold the good news till she got to Germany and give me a surprise. What about Sea Gull? I'd be really mad at her if she was applying for an American visa without telling me.

The next day my friend Jack Wong came over for dinner and mentioned that Sea Gull had been writing to him since he mailed her the application form. "Your sister is so warm and sweet," he said, licking his lips as if he were tasting her. "Even when she's depressed by her failure on the TOEFL, she's still considerate and understanding. We must help her."

"How?" I tried to look casual. "I've done all I can. If she can't come as a student, she can try as a tourist. I've sent her two kinds of forms. But I don't think her chances are good."

"That's why she needs help. I just found out that your boyfriend knows a guy named Jim Bergson. He's a consul in the U.S. Embassy in Beijing. You should ask him to write to Jim. If Jim is willing to help, I'm sure your sister can get a visa."

What did Sea Gull say to Jack that charmed him so? He was surprisingly concerned for someone he'd never seen. She seemed to love my friends. In China I once introduced her to Lee, a German who I was going out with during his short visit to Beijing, and she started to secretly correspond with him. At least she thought it was secret. Lee told me everything. My ex-boyfriend wrote to me in May that Sea Gull had begged him to sponsor her to come to Canada. He was frustrated, as he understood that she needed the help, but unfortunately he couldn't help her much. The responsibility was too much, and he couldn't afford supporting her, although he liked her a lot. Sometimes Sea Gull reminded me of the seeds of the Chinese forget-me-not; once they attached themselves to an object, it was hard to get rid of them. Unfortunately, she always stuck to the wrong object. Jack had no money at all to be her sponsor or provide her with room and board or pay for her tuition.

I wrote to her and demanded the truth. Her letter, which arrived a month later, made me regret having been harsh to her. She had failed the TOEFL by five points. She had applied for a tourist passport from the police station, but chickened out at the gate of the U.S. Embassy. "I should have tried, Sister," she wrote, "even though my friends told me the guards wouldn't let me in with an expired affidavit. But I was afraid to be rejected and afraid to tell you. This is only part of the reason I didn't write to you. I've been feeling horrible recently. I was cheated and betrayed by my boyfriend and my own sister. Sea Cloud went to Germany with my boyfriend, can you believe it? When Sea Cloud was homeless, I took her to Beijing and found her a job in my boyfriend's company. Sea Cloud kept telling me that he was no good, that he fooled around too much. I almost believed her. But I had never suspected that they would get together after I was exiled from Beijing. What pissed me off the most was that he still claimed I was the one he loved the best, that he missed me day and night in Germany, and that his feelings toward Sea Cloud were just those of sympathy, nothing else. He asked me to forgive him and be patient with him. As

soon as he settled down there, he'd bring me to Germany, too.
If it were true, then what was he doing with Sea Cloud in Kiel?
I still can't believe that my own sister would hurt me so badly,
that my boyfriend, after our five years of passionate and secre-
tive love, would have done this to me."

I couldn't believe it either. Was Sea Cloud really so desperate
that she stole Sea Gull's lover to get out of China? I was relieved
that she hadn't written to me. I wouldn't have known how to
deal with her. I didn't want to judge her, but it was hard not to.
What she had done to Sea Gull just didn't fit into the new image
she had given me on the ship from Shanghai to Dinghai—frag-
ile and helpless, yet understanding and beautiful in the moon-
light. It hurt me that she kept things from me while asking me
to sponsor her to come to America. I tried my best to console
Sea Gull, telling her that the man didn't deserve her. She
should feel lucky to get rid of such a heartless playboy.

"Come to America," I wrote. "I'm sending you another
affidavit and bank statement so that you can apply for admission the following semester. At the same time, you must pass
the English test. I'm sure you can do it. Prove to that guy that
you can do something without his help. I might be able to contact someone in the u.s. Embassy. If he's willing to help you, I'm
sure you can get a visa. By the way, why did you say your relationship with that guy was a secret? Something fishy about it. Is
he a married man?"

"Yes, he is," Sea Gull admitted in her letter, "and he has a son.
I knew it was wrong. But every time I made up my mind to
leave, he threatened to kill himself. I was helpless, Sister, and I
wish I were as strong and independent as you. Actually I
wouldn't have been so mad if Sea Cloud had told me the truth.
I would have congratulated them and wished them good luck.
I knew Sea Cloud needed more help. I just couldn't stand that

everyone in our family, even Mother and Grandma, kept away from me as if I had a disease. They fussed over Sea Cloud when she was waiting for her visa as if she were a queen. They all knew who was taking her to Germany, but no one told me what was going on until both he and Sea Cloud, separately, wrote to me from Kiel asking for forgiveness. I still remember I was the only one who offered Sea Cloud help when she was kicked out of her husband's place. Our family worships the winner and throws stones at the loser."

I was shocked that Sea Gull had been involved with a married man. To me, she seems cool and practical, always confident of what she is doing. She is the youngest, but our friends often said that Sea Gull looked like a mature older sister. She had won three championships for a provincial swimming team. She cooked well, designed and made her own clothing. She was an excellent ballroom dancer, a mathematician and accountant. But that was all I knew about her. When she was two years old, my parents sent her to live with Waipo. We spent a few weeks together only in summers. By the time she came to Dinghai to live with her family, I was already a freshman studying English at Bejing Foreign Language Institute. I used to think she was the luckiest girl in our family: I would have given away all I had to get away from my parents and live with my grandma.

I was very sympathetic to her but could say nothing. I guess Waipo and Mother kept it secret because they didn't want to hurt Sea Gull too much and also because they wanted to make sure that Sea Cloud left China safely. I sent two checks to Sea Gull, one for Queens College to revalidate her file when she passed the test, and the other for taking the TOEFL again. I advised her to apply to Queens College because they only required 500 for the TOEFL score while others wanted 550.

I thought I would hear from Sea Cloud soon. She had promised to write when she had accomplished something, and I figured getting herself to Germany counted as an accomplishment. Three months passed by without hearing one word from her. I asked Mother, Grandma, and Sea Gull about her, and they all said they hadn't heard from her either. Sea Gull said that she had moved several times since she arrived in Germany and now she had lost track of her. I was worried as well as annoyed. The guy she was living with wasn't trustworthy, and she didn't speak any German.

One early April morning, around three o'clock, Sea Cloud called. She was choked with sobs when she uttered *Sister.*

"The man gave you a hard time?" I said when she calmed down.

"He cursed me every day, even hit me when he was drunk. He made me go out looking for jobs at night and took all the money I made to pay for his tuition and drinks. I don't mind working, but I can't stand it when he takes my money and tells me I'm useless and lazy. He often threatens to send me back to China. I don't care any more. It's meaningless." She started sobbing again.

"Come to America," I said, conscious of having spoken these words so many times as if they were the only solution in life.

I don't know what to do anymore. Sometimes I think I'll just marry some rich old man, if anyone would have me, and live peacefully for the rest of my life. I'm too tired.

"Come to America," I repeated.

She stopped sobbing. "Do you think I can make it, Sister? I really don't want to disappoint you."

I think it's easier to get a visa from the u.s. Embassy in Germany than the one in Beijing. I'll send you an affidavit tomorrow. Give me your address."

"Thank you, Sister. I promise I'll learn English fast. I can speak some German already. Not as hard as I thought. And I learned to cook and clean houses. Here's my address: Dampferhofstraße 17, West Germany. Got it, Sister? I have to hang up. He's coming back. Bye, Sister."

I held the phone until the operator's taped voice came on. Sea Cloud was scared of the man. It was humiliating to accept the fact. She used to be so fearless! She used to take me around when she felt happy and generous with me and introduced me to her friends. She had so many friends, young and old, poor and rich, and they all adored her. Now she was even afraid of making a phone call. What would he do to her when the phone bill came? I looked at the address: Dampferhofstraße 17. Shit, she had forgotten to give me the city name. But I still got together affidavit and bank statement the next day, and mailed them registered, hoping the German post office would return the letter to me if they couldn't find her.

A month later, Sea Cloud sent me a pair of earrings inside the envelope. "For you, Sister," she wrote:

> Yesterday the old lady I worked for slipped fifty marks into my pocket. I ran out and bought these with the money. Thank you so much for the document. It was delayed two weeks because I gave you an incomplete address. Reading your letter was almost as good as seeing you in person. I'll go to the u.s. Embassy as soon as possible. But right now I depend on this man to extend my visa. I came here pretending I was his wife. His wife and son are still in Beijing, waiting for him to bring them to Germany. They don't know anything about his affairs. I cook for him during the day, and carry newspapers at night. It's hard to get jobs since Germany has been reunited. I don't have a

working permit and can work only at night, illegally. I make about six hundred marks a month. He takes it all and asks me why I make so little. I'm looking for a job in a restaurant so that I'll have some cash for my escape. Don't send me any money, Sister, because he opens the mail. If I can't make enough for the airplane fare, I'll steal some from his bank account. I know where he puts his bank card, and I know his secret access code. When he had just gotten the card, he didn't know how to use the machine and asked somebody for help. I overheard him mention the code number and memorized it. It's 7474. It's my money too. I'm learning fast, Sister. Suffering is good for me. It has made me tough. Sometimes I'm even happy, especially when I think of the things I'll be able to do in future. When I was in China, everything was planned by our parents and the government. I often felt stifled and helpless. Maybe this is why everyone wants to go abroad.

Love,

Sea Cloud

P.S. His name is Zhang. He seduced Sea Gull when she was his student. He was still single then. After he got married, he still wouldn't let her go. He had tons of girlfriends and often visited the red-light district. Sea Gull rejected many good men for Zhang. I told her to leave him, but she wouldn't listen. When Zhang turned his attention to me, I accepted him just to help Sea Gull get rid of the rascal. I was a divorced woman. I didn't care. But Sea Gull must have her future. I couldn't let her bind herself to him all her life. Sea

Gull isn't talking to me right now. But someday she'll understand and thank me.

My boyfriend asked me why I was in a bad mood. I told him briefly about the story. He got very excited and said he'd fly to Germany to beat up the guy and bring Sea Cloud to America. I pointed out to him that he couldn't do anything for my sister unless he married her and got her a green card. Unfortunately he was still legally married to his second wife, although they had been separated for years.

"What can you do then? You can't let her be enslaved there, alone," he said sharply, annoyed at being reminded of his marriage status.

"Nothing else to do but wait. I've sent her an affidavit."

"That's all you can do, eh, affidavit."

I walked away quickly so I wouldn't throw a chair at him. I was mad because he had said the truth, and the truth hurt. My sisters were suffering, yet I could do nothing to help them except send them those useless papers.

On a muggy August day, I was having tea with my Chinese friends in the backyard of an Italian bar. It was our monthly meeting to edit our Chinese poetry magazine. After a while, our topic turned to the Albanians who had recently swarmed onto an old ship, trying to get into Italy. Someone commented that he would never enter a hostile country just to make some money.

"It's not just for money," I interrupted him. "When people are willing to put up with such hardship and humiliation, and even risk their lives, it means they're seeking something more than money."

"Maybe you're right," my friend said, not very pleased at

being interrupted. He was the editor of the magazine, and I was the only female in the poetry circle. Since I had produced little, I was generally regarded as a fan, a volunteer worker. "But what about the Chinese women? All they think about is how to marry Western men so as to come to America. Even those who come here with their husbands soon run away with rich old American guys for a better life. You can't deny that, right? These two guys here," he pointed to the two young poets on my right, "can tell you how their wives just left them."

I remained silent. I didn't want to have a fight with them, my only Chinese connection. But how I wished I could remind them that Chinese women had to go through many more difficulties than men! I suddenly remembered my sisters. Sea Cloud was still waiting patiently for her escape to Hamburg to apply for an American visa. Sea Gull had completely given up after her second failure at the TOEFL, refusing to communicate with anyone in the family. I dared not tell her that my connection in the embassy was gone. My boyfriend's friend, Jim the consul, had apologized in his letter for not being able to help. There were too many Chinese applying to go to America. Mother was worried that Sea Gull might do something terrible to herself.

"Help her," she urged me. "Only you can do it now. Find her a husband in America. It doesn't matter what he does as long as he has a green card. We can't let her be buried in that remote backwater for the rest of her life."

LOTUS

☞ After I soaked my feet in hot water for half an hour, I lifted my left foot near my eyes under the dim table lamp and trimmed it carefully with scissors. So ugly. Hard yellow dead skin on the heel, the side of the toe, and the sole, a result of being squeezed into cheap artificial leather shoes. Were they really my own feet? I wondered why Chinese called women's feet "lotuses." Mine were like dead fish, but they looked nice in tight shoes. I cast a sidelong glance at the long line of shoes along the wall. It is said that female Leos love shoes. True. Six pairs of leather shoes, four pairs of sandals, two pairs of boots, four pairs of sneakers, high-, middle-, and low-heeled, white, black, brown, blue, gray, pink. . . . A familiar funny smell came from the foot. Yes, Nainai's feet smelled the same way. For fifteen years, I'd been watching her unbinding the six-foot-long, two-inch-wide ribbon from her feet, then soaking her three-inch long feet in hot water. Steam with that smell rose from the basin.

"Nainai, why do you have only one toe on each of your feet? Where are the others?"

"Oh, they hide themselves under the soles."

She lifted her feet. Ai! the eight small toes were mercilessly bent deep into the soles. The heels, being the only good part of the feet, had become unnaturally big and strong compared to the pointed one-toe front. I touched the toes and withdrew quickly. They were dead, the bones broken inside and the flesh helplessly attached to the sole.

"Hurt, Nainai?"

"Of course. But this is nothing compared to the pain when I just started to bind my feet at the age of six. Mom forced me to walk around with a bamboo stick. I heard my toe bones cracking and breaking under my soles with each step. Soon my feet swelled, festered, and yellow pus oozed out between the ribbons. I couldn't sleep at night. I begged Mom to free my feet. Mom held me in her arms, crying, 'Poor daughter, forgive Mom. It's all for your good. No man wants a girl with natural big feet.' I cried, too, and promised her never to complain again."

She smiled proudly, and was quiet for a while.

"Finally I had a pair of 'three-inch golden lotuses,' well known in my hometown. A rich man married me, your grandfather, and he died when your father was only six."

"Why is it called *lotus*, Nainai?"

She sat in silence as if she hadn't heard my question. Suddenly she jumped off the bed. "I have something to show you."

From the bottom of her trunk, she took out a pair of shoes. At first, I took them for toys. They were delicate, small, soft, and cute. No longer than my hand. As I held them, I suddenly had an urge to bite them and keep them in my mouth. Ah, that was why men called them lotuses. I looked at the shoes and at my own feet. I was eight years old but already had extremely big feet, size six. Ai, how ugly! Mother would yell whenever she bought me shoes. I wasn't ashamed then. But now, in front of Granny's lotuses, I was no longer proud of my big feet. Quietly,

I found two strips of wide elastic cord and bound my feet. I told Mother to buy me shoes smaller than my feet, though I had to clench my teeth to push my feet into them. I succeeded. My feet remained size six.

Last year I happened to see a pair of embroidered lotus shoes in my American friend's house in Brooklyn. They bought them in Gui Lin, a southwestern city in China, in the summer of 1986. There they saw a woman carried by her husband. She couldn't walk by herself because her bound feet were only three inches long.

"Oh, she must be very old," I said casually.

"No, she looked to be in her thirties."

A young woman with bound feet at the end of the twentieth century! For a while, I couldn't utter a word. Then I laughed. No reason to be shocked. Hadn't I worn small shoes to stop my feet from growing? Weren't so many women, Asian and Western, still wearing high-heeled shoes in order to look sexy, in spite of the pain and bad consequences? I remembered once in a Chinese bookstore I found a book with pictures of Chinese men playing Golden Lotuses. The most beautiful feet must meet the following seven standards: agile, slim, bending, small, soft, straight, and fragrant.

Fragrant? As the scissors dug deeper behind the nails to pick out dead skin, the smell got worse. I sighed. I loved sneakers and flat-heeled shoes, for they were much more comfortable. Still, I would rather wear high-heeled shoes to look nicer. I suffered voluntarily. A modern lotus.

But for whom and what? I shook my head. Even if I could answer the question, I would continue doing the same thing. So what was the point of giving myself a headache at midnight? When I finally finished the work to beautify myself, I put some lotion on my feet to make them fragrant, and turned off the light.

SONG
OF
FOUR
SEASONS

☞ The hubbub in the concert hall of the Kinghaven Music School suddenly stopped when the audience in the balcony started singing at the same time as if conducted by an invisible conductor. I was surrounded by the voices that seemed to be coming from above, my left and right, and behind me. I looked up timidly at the singers. They looked so young and carefree, leaning on the rails of the balcony and singing without self-consciousness. Some of them stuck their bare feet through the rails and dangled them out casually in the air. I sat motionless, hypnotized by their swaying pink soles and siren song. A sudden rage, mingled with awe and hopeless desire, submerged me.

Music, especially live music played on a violin or piano, or sung by a choir, always had that effect on me. Maybe it was because I heard real music too late and too suddenly, and it has made me a little bit crazy ever since.

I was fifteen, then, and was to become a peasant in Lishao Village in a week. That day, after dinner, I took a basin of dirty dishes to the public tap downstairs. The apartment we had moved into four months ago had no sink or bathroom. It didn't even have a kitchen. I cooked in the hallway. On the way I stopped at the backyard that had been divided into chicken coops. The fading light of dusk reflected off the steel cages along the western wall. The shabby coops looked beautiful in the rays of the sunset. The chickens jumped up and down as they saw me with a basin, their feathers sparkling in the orange light. I walked to the coop that belonged to my family and scraped the leftover rice into the trough. There were four hens and one rooster. The snow white rooster weighed about twelve pounds. After he had defeated the rest of the roosters in the yard, he patronized all the hens, and even attacked any human that dared touch them. I had to keep him locked up except when some neighbors wanted him to mate with their hens.

Gloomily, I watched my chickens gobbling up chunks of fried bean curd. That was my share of dinner that I didn't touch. Mother didn't exactly forbid me to eat, but she didn't call me to the table at dinnertime and nobody else dared say anything. It was fine with me. Even if I had had an appetite, I couldn't eat: my front teeth were all loose, my lips swollen, and my nose stuffed with cotton to stop the bleeding. I had scraped my chest and my face against the edge of the windowsill when mother pulled me down by my ankles. It all happened so fast. I was cleaning the windows and thinking about my future in the countryside when I heard the piercing howl. Before I could turn to find out what had happened, I was on the floor. Mother was jumping around me, cursing, crying, slapping me and herself with the music sheets I had used to clean the windows. I was too baffled and scared to feel the pain. Mother was bad tempered, and often hit and cursed her children, but I had never seen her go crazy like this. I must have done something terrible.

"You, you, you," she hissed, pointing at me with the sheets, "you are my nightmare, my *ke xing,* my killing star, my bad luck.

You have ruined my life. You have destroyed my last hope. Old heaven, what have I done to you? Why did you punish me with such a daughter?" She threw the sheet on my back and ran into her bedroom.

I sat up, gathered the dirty sheets, which I had wrinkled into balls after I had cleaned the windows, and flattened them one by one. Blood trickled down my nose and dripped on the white paper. The drops of blood looked like flowers in an ink painting. I had pulled out a carton from under Mother's bed, hoping to find some used notebook paper with which to clean the windows. The box was filled with Mao's collected books and copies of *Red Flag* magazine. I wouldn't touch those books. I had heard enough stories about those who were jailed for defacing Mao's portrait and his writings. At the bottom, I found something peculiar. Instead of words, strange sproutlike signs crawled all over the pages. On the cover, it said "Violin Score of Beethoven's Fate Symphony (the Fifth Symphony)." I didn't know who Beethoven was, but I was awed by the mysteriousness of the signs and the fine paper. It must be Mother's old stuff that had escaped the Red Guards' confiscation in the beginning of the Cultural Revolution. I didn't even know that Mother played violin. I stroked the fine paper, wondering if I should use it to clean the windows. I looked up and saw the twelve pieces of dirty glass, then remembered the dinner I had to prepare for the family, and I made the decision. I tore off five pages and climbed onto the windowsill.

When I flattened the last sheet, a vertical line of characters jumped out at me: "For daughter Shen Chen, who won the first prize in the high school graduation violin contest." It was signed by Waigong, my grandpa. My stomach cramped. No wonder Mother was so upset. But how on earth could I have known the value of the book since I hardly had any musical education? Except for a few children songs I had learned from

Mother at the elementary school, all I knew were "Red Is the East," "The Internationale," "Chop the Heads of the Japanese Ghosts with Our Sabres," and the eight reformed Beijing Operas. They were just slogans and hysterical screams; at best, they sounded like angry desperate curses. Besides, I hadn't even seen a violin in my life. Was I really her bad luck as she had said? I trembled at the thought that had been running through my mind for a long time: Mother didn't like me. Mother had never wanted me.

"Your chickens are really beautiful, Seaweed," someone said behind my back. I jumped up and saw Yaxian. She lived two doors away from me, in a suite with three big bedrooms, a real kitchen, a private sink, and a telephone. Her father was the head of the operational department in the East China Sea Navy Base. It was said that he was going to be promoted soon and his family would move to a more luxurious compound for high-ranking officials. Mother was bitter that her husband hadn't been promoted for the past eight years. With his years of service in the Navy, he should have had a higher rank than Yaxian's father. She didn't allow us to play with other kids in the compound. They were either urchins or snobs, she told us. Since my family moved here, I hadn't made any friends.

"Do you want to pet the rooster? He won't bite you when I'm around," I offered. I liked her immediately because she praised my chickens.

She smiled and shook her head. "I've heard you're going to the countryside soon. Is that true?"

I nodded my head slowly. My heart sank as I saw the pity in her eyes. For the first time I began to feel nervous about my new life. I was going to be on my own in a very poor village. Everything would be completely different and difficult. Could I handle it? Once I became a peasant, I would lose my city residence and wouldn't be able to come back unless the Party secretary in the people's commune believed I had been well reeducated and recommended me to colleges or factories if there were any openings. But what if I wasn't recommended? I didn't want to think about it and squatted to collect the scattered dishes on the ground.

"What are you going to do with your chickens?" Yaxian squatted next to me and asked with concern. "Nobody can raise them as well as you."

"I don't know." I was growing more depressed as I thought about the fate of my chickens. "I'll try to take some with me if possible. My mother likes to eat chicken and it costs a lot to buy them. Maybe it's better for them that way. Everyone in my family likes chicken meat, but no one remembers feeding them on time or cleaning the coop. It's better to die than suffer."

As if they could understand our conversation, the chickens stopped pecking at the food and stared at us with their unblinking eyes. I picked up the dishes and was going to leave when Yaxian said, "Seaweed, I'm going to No. 3 Navy Compound to visit a friend. Would you like to go with me? He has a gramophone and some old records."

I stood stiff with disbelief. It was the first time I had ever been invited anywhere since I moved here. For a moment, I thought she was making fun of me, something the children from higher-rank families liked to do to the children whose fathers were in lower positions. I looked down at my toes, which stuck out of my shoes, then covered my broken face with my hand.

"I can help you wash the dishes," she said. I looked up into her eyes. Her brown eyes were warm and sincere. I noticed she was actually good-looking. Her tall big-boned body no longer intimidated me, and the freckles on her nose were so cute that I wanted to touch them with my fingertips. I untied my apron and threw it on the dishes.

"Let's go," I said.

"How about the dishes? How about your mother? She'll look for you if you don't tell her where you're going."

I waved my hand to brush my mother away. Mother would never let me go out with Yaxian. If I went back to ask her permission, I'd lose the chance once and for all. Once she said no, I wouldn't have the guts to disobey her. The best thing to do was go with Yaxian and have a good time. I'd worry about the punishment later.

I followed Yaxian into No. 3 compound and up the newly-painted stairways. It was neat and quiet here. There were no stoves, no wood or coal balls in baskets, no other kitchen supplies outside each family's door along the hallway. I heard that each apartment had a spacious kitchen and their orderlies came daily to clean and shop for the officers and their families. Yaxian's father also had an orderly. Every morning, at ten o'clock, he would pass by my family's kitchen with a full basket of vegetables and meat in his hand. Our kitchen was on the landing outside our apartment. When he came upstairs, I was always cooking on the coal stove, and had to stand against the wall to let him pass. Though we had never talked to each other, I felt we were linked by our common misfortune. Neither of us was doing what we wanted to do. He was supposed to be on a Navy ship and I in a college classroom.

Yaxian stopped at the end of the hallway and knocked on the door of Room 204. I heard music playing inside. It stopped at the sound of our knocking. Both the melody and the instrument were alien to me, yet I felt I had heard them a long time ago in my dreams. The sound stayed in my ears like the aftertaste of new spring green tea. The door opened. A slender man in his twenties smiled at us and gestured to invite us in. He was the most handsome man I'd ever seen. I was so dazzled by his white shirt and white teeth that I dared not look at his face. Yaxian introduced him as Fang. But my full attention was on the musical instrument he had been holding gracefully under his chin. "Violin," I whispered. I'd never seen one, but I knew what it was. Fang heard my whisper and held it out to me with a smile. I almost fainted with disbelief and excitement. But instead of taking it, I plucked a string gently with my fingers. The sound it made startled me. I looked up, and all of us laughed merrily.

Fang led us into another room, where all the windows were covered with thick velvet curtains. He hung his violin on the wall and pulled out a gramophone and a box of records from under his bed. He moved around noiselessly like a cat. I noticed how well preserved his hands were. So were Yaxian's hands, although her complexion was bad. They had never washed a dish or made coal balls from coal powder. Both of their families had orderlies to do the dirty work in the household. I hid my hands under my thighs. They were ruined by frostbite. I also wished I had a gauze mask to cover my swollen lips.

The gramophone hissed softly as the record spun around. The jacket looked quite worn out and the record had tiny cracks in it. It was Beethoven's Fifth Symphony. I trembled as I recognized the name. It seemed that my day was in the hand of fate. The needle jumped slightly over a scratch and made a funny noise. Suddenly the music began. It sounded like a spirit knocking on the door at midnight. It knocked once, twice— persisting, demanding, terrifying—then entered me, whirled around and pulled my heart with its tender hands. I sat still, but all the organs in my body were stirred up, pushing and screaming against each other in order to get out. Tears gathered in my eyes. I felt a deep sorrow, yet I had never felt so fulfilled. Yaxian buried her head between her knees. Fang looked up at the ceiling as if listening to a call from heaven, his hand inserted in his long hair. No one moved or said anything after the music stopped. Then Fang gently put the record and the gramophone back and closed the trunk. Yaxian stood up to leave. I didn't move. I wanted to hold onto the new world a bit longer. I wasn't ready to go back to the dirty dishes yet. Yaxian murmured something to Fang. He nodded, took down the violin from the wall and began to play.

I had never heard a violin before. The sound flowed from the strings like a sobbing stream. Yaxian hummed along with the song Fang played. Although I didn't know anything about it, I could tell it wasn't Beethoven or any other Western composer. It must be an old Chinese song since Yaxian knew the words. Unlike the Fate Symphony, which had just crashed into me like a shooting star, leaving a huge crater in my body, this music filled the hole with soothing water and solid earth, gently and patiently. It repeated four times.

I left Fang's place in a trance, forgetting to thank him, forgetting to say good-bye to Yaxian. The only thing I could hear was the knocking of fate in Beethoven's Fifth Symphony and the song; the only thing I could see were the violin, Fang's beautiful fingers moving along the strings, and his chin on the base.

I didn't even panic when I discovered that the dishes I had left next to the coop were gone and the door was chained from the inside. I knocked on the window of the kids' room. My sister Sea Cloud whispered through the crack, "What happened to you? Are you out of your mind? Did you eat a leopard's gallbladder? Mother looked for you the whole night. She was so furious even her nostrils had smoke. She said no one was to let you in tonight."

Fine with me. I really didn't want to confront Mother right now. I wasn't afraid of her punishment, at least not tonight, but I did fear that her screaming would ruin the sensation the music had created in me. I wanted to hold onto it as long as possible. Sitting on the floor against the door, I settled down for the night.

At dawn, Father opened the door and let me in. I walked straight into Mother's room, my heart steeled with resolution. I thought to myself, "Tell her the truth and get it over with. Whatever she'll do to me doesn't matter anymore. Soon I'll be on my own."

Mother sat on the edge of the bed. She looked as if she were going to teach me a lesson that I'd not forget for the rest of my life. But instead of cursing me as usual, she stared at me in silence for such a long time that my knees trembled. At that moment, I understood the old Chinese custom of kneeling in front of their parents. Perhaps it was much easier to avoid and cool a mother's wrath by throwing oneself on the floor and burying one's head in one's hands.

"Well, say something about yourself," Mother finally opened her mouth.

"I went to No. 3 Navy Compound with Yaxian," I said, my tone completely void of remorse and guilt. Mother's body stiffened inside her loose robe, as if she had been struck by some invisible stone. She was ready to burst at any moment. I continued desperately, "We listened to music—Beethoven's Fate Symphony—on her friend's gramophone."

She collapsed as I uttered the name Beethoven. Her shoulders drooped, and her head bent like a sick chicken. All the spirit and power drained from her body. I wanted to say something, but didn't know how. I had never seen Mother like this. Finally she sighed. "Next time, let me know where you are if you want to go out. Go to bed now and get some sleep."

I stood still. I couldn't believe Mother had let me go so easily. But she had stretched out again on her bed, her eyes closed, her hair floating above the white pillow. I moved quietly to the kids' room. Before I reached the door, she called me, "Seaweed!"

I turned sharply toward her. I knew it. She had pretended to let me go to make me relax, then she would punish me, just to make her power more terrible.

"Seaweed," Mother lifted her upper body to look me in the eyes. "You'll leave for the countryside in a week. I think you should visit your friends, your teachers, and old classmates to say good-bye. I'll tell Sea Cloud to wash dishes after supper from now on, so that you can go out in the evening."

For the rest of the days before I left home, I put down my bowl after dinner and walked out under my sister's jealous eye. I never visited any friend, because I had none, and I didn't feel like seeing my teachers. What could we say to each other? They had put so much hope in me, believing that if anyone could go to college, it would be me. I had believed so too. But I was going to the countryside instead. I had failed, although it wasn't my fault, because I had never been given a chance even to compete. So better to leave the town as quietly as possible.

For five evenings, I sat in a dark corner of No. 3 Navy Compound. Nothing happened on the first three nights. Then I heard him play, something monotonous and repetitious, with constant halts and errors; but to me, it was the most delicious, heavenly music on earth. My three days of waiting were nothing. It was the price to pay for this delight. On the fifth day, however, he didn't play. No light came out of his room. I waited, telling myself that I'd be rewarded for my patience and belief. Finally I dozed off, only to be awakened by footsteps on the staircase. Two people appeared on the second-floor porch. It was Fang and a young woman. He opened the door, turned on the light, and pulled the woman into his arms, right on the threshold. The woman had two "revolutionary brushes" hanging over her shoulders. Her dark hair made her face look unnaturally white. She threw her head backward, her lips parted slightly to receive his kiss.

I walked home like a zombie. I felt both empty and overwhelmed at the same time. The deep itch inside me, which had been pacified by Fang's violin for the past week, started to act up again and made my soul restless and crazy. Mother was bending over the bed, sewing a quilt. I passed by her without a word. No one was in the kids' room. My sister and brother hadn't come home yet. I sat on the bed trying to read. But the words turned into musical notes laughing at my blindness. Tears dropped on the book.

Mother came in with the finished quilt. She put it on the bed and said, "For you. I added two jin of new cotton. Should keep you warm in winter. You've packed, yes? Your father has arranged a jeep for tomorrow afternoon. He won't be able to go, since he's leaving tomorrow morning for Shanghai on business. But Sea Cloud and I will go with you."

I nodded, my head bent deep to hide my wet cheeks. Mother touched my shoulder. "Your hair got loose. Turn over. I'll braid it for you."

Mother combed my hair with her horn comb, which she always placed on top of her dresser. So she had noticed my loosened braids when I passed her room and had come into my room to do my hair. As the comb scraped my scalp, I trembled with pleasure. Mother's fingers raked through my hair, so gently, the full length of my hair, which reached below my buttocks. Each strand of hair felt the warmth of her fingers. The last time she had combed my hair was ten years ago, when I was five years old, when I came to live with her for the first time since I had been born. The two braids that Waipo had made for me on the day of my departure loosened when I got off the ship with Mother. My hair was all tangled and knotted together. I tried to braid it but my fingers didn't listen to me. Mother brushed my hair with her black hairbrush. It was my first day of school and I needed to look neat. I screamed in pain as soon as those iron teeth touched—no, bit into—my head. Mother cursed and stamped her feet. She was already late for work. She grabbed a pair of scissors and eliminated the tangles and knots in two minutes. "No more long hair in my house," she declared, "unless you are old enough to do it yourself." She put me on the back seat of her bike and rushed me off to school. I sobbed silently in the back, trying not to touch her. The haircut made me feel naked and bald-headed. How I missed Waipo!

"There, two braids. Take a look at my skill." She handed me her mirror, the only one in the family. She had thought of everything. "You have very thick hair, just like me. Only yours is much stronger. Are you sure you don't want to cut it before you leave? It'll be most inconvenient once you start working in the fields."

I shook my head slightly. The mirror reflected two faces. Mother looked so young and beautiful. She had a round face, large expressive eyes, and a straight delicate nose that turned up a little at the end. My face, so long and skinny, was unfortunately matched with small eyes and a big nose. My two thick braids hanging beside my ears looked unreal. No one believed that I was her daughter when we walked together on the streets. Mother took the mirror away from my hand.

"It's eight-thirty, not too late. Come on, Seaweed, put on your shoes. I want to show you something."

She lifted her bicycle on her shoulder and walked downstairs. I followed her, wondering where she was taking me, and how. Mother hardly went out in the evening since she liked to go to sleep early, around ten. The place she wanted to take me must be far, otherwise she wouldn't have needed her bike. But what about me? I was not going to run after her while she pedaled. Mother patted the back seat and said, "Sit here."

"No, no, mother." I backed away a few steps. "I'm too heavy for you."

"No problem. You can't be heavier than your sister. I take her around all the time. Hurry up, the school gate will be locked soon."

I got on the bike, my body as stiff as a crooked branch on a dead tree. My hands didn't know where to go. Usually I put my arms around the rider's waist to keep my balance. But I couldn't imagine doing this to Mother. We had never been this close to each other: her back brushed my right shoulder rhythmically as she pedaled with a steady speed, and her smell—a faint musk odor from her favorite soap—stimulated my nostrils and made me sneeze. It was too much for me. I'd rather run after the bike. I was about to say something when Mother went over a crack in the street. "Hold onto me," she shouted. I grabbed her waist. A big bump, but we stayed up. Mother's flesh was soft. Through her cotton jacket, a stream of warmth flowed into my open palm from her body. It relaxed me immediately. I adjusted my position on the back seat to make myself more comfortable.

Soon we arrived at Dinghai Middle School. The old man was closing the gate, but let us in without asking questions when he saw Mother. She leaned the bicycle against the wall of the main building and took me down to the basement. She undid the iron lock and walked in. I followed her, wondering why Mother had a key to such a room. Piled up against the walls were antique desks and chairs, some of the legs broken, but the beautiful carvings and designs still recognizable under the thick layer of dust. In the middle stood a giant piano, sealed with a strip of white paper with a black character *feng* (sealed) and the official red seal of the Revolutionary Committee of Dinghai Middle School, dated September 15, 1967. There was an organ behind the piano. When I was in elementary school, Mother had been my music teacher until she was transferred to this middle school. I still remembered the children's songs and revolutionary songs she had taught us on the organ. I had always thought it was the most elegant, the grandest musical instrument in the world. But the piano made it look like a comical dwarf. On top of the organ was an accordion. I immediately recognized it. Mother had taken it home several times to teach Sea Cloud how to sing. She inherited Mother's sweet voice.

Mother pulled a nearby bench up to the piano and sat down. Then she lifted the cover without the slightest hesitation. My heart stopped beating for a moment, then bumped against my throat violently. Mother must be mad. The seal broke with a thud, kicked up some dust, and hung limply over the side. Mother swept her hands, first her right, then her left, over the keys. So this was the sound a piano made, like a crystal river running swiftly through a desert, a handful of pearls falling on a green jade plate, a thousand kids running into the blue ocean, their chubby legs splashing about in the foamy water. I stood spellbound, my mouth wide open, waiting for more.

Mother lifted her hands in the air for a few seconds, looked in my direction, nodded at me, then started to play. It was slow and sounded very familiar. I listened carefully. Yes, I had heard Fang play this song on his violin. Before I could say something, Mother began to sing:

When spring comes,
peach blossoms cover the front yard.
Sister sits under the window,
embroidering a pair of mandarin ducks on a pipe pouch.

When summer comes,
lotuses lift their pink lips above the lake.
Ducks swim shoulder to shoulder among the green leaves,
and Sister hears the footsteps of her lover.

When autumn comes,
the west wind turns leaves red and yellow.
A thunderstorm dispersed the ducks in all directions,
cannons called Sister's brother to fight the Japanese ghosts.

Mother stopped singing. I was weeping, my face buried in the dust that had gathered on the piano for seven years. It was too much for me to bear: the music, the song, the feeling of regret for leaving home and Mother for a strange place, the feeling of guilt for destroying Mother's music notebook, and finally, Mother's affection. I was ashamed of crying in front of her, but at the same time, I felt strangely relieved. Mother loved me after all. Otherwise, she wouldn't have chosen to sing that song for me, just for me. She put her hand on the back of my head. Again, I felt that incredible sensation of warmth and closeness.

She lifted my head and cleaned my face with her white handkerchief. A shadow of sadness clouded her eyes as she touched my swollen lips with her fingertips.

"Hurt still?"

I shook my head. I wanted to tell her how sorry I was to tear her Beethoven into pieces, but the words came out as a question, "What's for winter?"

She looked at me, then smiled mysteriously. "Depends. It could be despair and death, or it could be rest and hope. You have to decide for yourself, Seaweed."

I nodded. Mother closed the lid and stood up to leave. At the door, I turned to take a last look at the piano. The seal, once it was broken, looked weak and comical. The room still echoed with the sound of the piano and Mother's sweet voice. I suddenly said loudly, "It must be 'Song of Four Seasons' then."

She said nothing, but wrapped her arm around my shoulders. It was at that moment that I made two wishes.

The singing in the concert hall came to a sudden halt. I sat up on my bench in this eerie silence to see what was going on. On the stage, which took up almost half of the auditorium, four men were still moving around a grand piano, and two teenage girls, apparently the students of the summer music school, were arranging wine glasses and jars on a stand next to the piano under the supervision of a moustachioed man in his late forties. The concert wasn't going to start for a while. The audience resumed their conversations. I looked to my left. My boyfriend was whispering something to Maria. She laughed, her head thrown backward, her arm over his shoulder. She had very long, slender fingers, like those of a pianist, elegant but nervous. The color of her nail polish—precisely red—matched her lipstick. Maria had just returned from Germany. The success of her first book in Europe had added a lot of power and charm to her voice and gestures. Her husband, Al, was one of the hottest fiction writers in America. He and Laura, also a successful novelist, were having a heated discussion on politics and art. Her husband, Glen, was staring into space on the other side of the long bench. He and I were the only nonwriters in this group. We had met Laura and Glen at a ski resort in Vermont through Maria and Al, whom we had encountered by accident in a Benneton outlet store a week before. When we discovered that we had rented our summer houses in the same town, we immediately arranged dinner parties and babysitters, movies and concerts. It was amazing how quickly we became intimate and how frequently we saw one another in the countryside. We lived only five blocks apart in the city, but rarely spent time together.

I tried not to look at Glen. His gloomy, confused eyes depressed me. Although he had blond hair and a red beard, I could tell he was also a foreigner in this country because he spoke English with a strong accent. I had to constantly tell myself that I should feel happy, that everything was working out for me: I had a two-year contract as a bilingual teacher in PS 1 in Manhattan, my salary was raised to almost $35,000 a year, my first summer house turned out to be a beauty (a sunny, three-story glass-and-wood building on a place called Devil's Hill, facing a pond and two private museums), and my boyfriend was a respected poet and novelist with seven published books to his name. I really had nothing to complain about.

Why did I have to remind myself to be happy?

The singing started again, first on the left balcony, then the right, then the back. The exuberant voices, fresh and unpretentious, pushed down to the middle where I was sitting, from above, from all directions, wave after wave, with the power of a full tide. I rolled over and over, choking; I swam with all my strength to rise above the water for a gasp of air, but the waves instantly pulled me down again. Finally, I stopped this futile struggle, my limbs too weak, my lungs already filled with water, and let the tide carry me down to the bottom of the sea.

I made two wishes when Mother put her arm around my shoulders: one was to learn how to play the violin and surprise Mother with the accomplishment, and the other was to buy a piano for her, a Mason & Hamlin, the kind Mother had played in that school basement. Both wishes needed money, especially the second one, which would be probably a lifelong project. So I decided to start with the violin.

During my first year in Lishao Village, the government gave

me ten yuan a month as a stipend because peasants didn't get monthly salaries. At the end of the year, the production team the peasants belonged to added up the points each worker had accumulated for the past year and paid them with rice, sweet potatoes, vegetables, and other products they had grown in the fields. The peasant women exchanged rice and eggs for other necessities like needles and thread, matches, soy sauce, and so on. They also raised chickens and pigs and sold them to the government for cash. I spent only one yuan each month on toilet paper, toothpaste, salt, and lard, saving the rest of the stipend. My production team advanced me two hundred jin of rice and a strip of land in someone's garden to grow vegetables. My mother gave me a hen and a duck. For three months, before the vegetables grew and the hen and duck laid eggs, I ate nothing but rice with salt and lard. When I thought of the money at the bottom of my trunk and the violin I was going to hold under my chin, the bland rice became the best delicacy imaginable.

When I received my eleventh stipend, I wrote a letter to my first aunt in Shanghai and said that my mother had asked her to buy a violin. I put the ten pink ten-yuan notes into the envelope and mailed it as a registered letter from the tiny post office of the people's commune.

It was during the next two months that I learned what waiting and despairing meant. In the beginning I counted time by weeks, then by days, then by hours and minutes. I couldn't sleep or eat. I was attacked by the thought that the mail was lost, that there was no violin available in Shanghai, or that it had gotten damaged in the mail. When I finally couldn't bear it anymore, I decided to go home. I hadn't seen my parents for almost a year. They had been asking me in their letters whether I'd return for the Spring Festival. I counted my money, just enough to buy a ticket for the four-hour bus ride.

When I arrived in the midafternoon, no one was home. I

opened the door with my old key. Everything remained the same: the kettle on the sealed coal stove, the food cover on the kitchen table, the bottles and books and mirror on Mother's dresser, her badly made bed, and . . . I stopped at the threshold between my parents' room and the kids' room, stunned. On the wall, above the bed my sister and I used to share, hung a violin! I stared at it with my mouth open. I held out my hand. It was so near yet beyond my reach. I couldn't understand why the violin I had waited for day and night for two months had ended up here.

Someone embraced me from my behind. "Hi, big sister, you're back!" It was Sea Cloud. She must have been delighted to see me, for she had never embraced me before, and hardly ever called me "big sister." But my body was too stiff to return her affection. The only thing I could do was point at the wall.

"Oh, that," she said indifferently, flinging her schoolbag on the bed, "I don't know what got into first aunt. She just sent this violin out of the blue, no letter, not even a note to explain why. Mom was mad. If first aunt wanted to make up with Mom for the fights they had had in the past, all she had to do was write a letter. But to spend so much money on this thing without a word of explanation, she must be crazy! The more Mom brooded on this, the angrier she became. She thought that first aunt sent her this violin to laugh at her. So she tossed it to me and told me it was mine. But what can I do with it? Mother doesn't want to teach me. I don't know anyone else who can and will teach me. Besides, I don't think I'm interested in it. Too complicated, too much work. But it doesn't look bad to have a violin on the wall, does it? It gives the room an artistic look."

I clenched my teeth to prevent myself from shouting or banging my head against the wall. I was such a fool to assume that my first aunt would send the violin to me since she and

Mother were not on speaking terms. Of course she wouldn't. First of all, I didn't even have an address. All the mail went to the office of the people's commune. When the Party secretary of each village went to have a meeting there, they picked up the letters and parcels and brought them back to the villagers. Besides, I wrote the letter in the name of my mother and made it look like it was my mother who wanted the violin, because I didn't want anyone to know that I had one hundred yuan and spent it on myself instead of giving it to my family.

I looked at the violin. With a black shoelace around its neck, and its base covered with dust, it had lost its sacredness. As I stared at it, something collapsed in me. I had made two wishes to please Mother, but my hard efforts seemed to have only turned me into a selfish, dishonest fool. I wasn't a good daughter, and probably never would be.

The singing in the auditorium reached its climax. Everyone joined in. The thunderous chorus seemed like it was going to pierce the roof at any moment. I couldn't figure out the words except for *love*. I repeated it to myself over and over, until I actually uttered the word *ai*. As soon as I realized what I was saying, I jumped from my seat. I had never said *love* in Chinese. No matter how hard my Chinese lovers pressed me, I insisted on saying "I love you" in English or French, arguing that it was much more romantic and exotic. But at the bottom of my heart, I knew I couldn't say it in Chinese, although I had no problem writing it in my letters. "Ai, ai, ai . . ." I uttered the word gently and repeatedly, for fear that I'd blow it away if I said it too loud, that I'd forget it if I stopped the repetition. How incredible! It took me thirty-five years to learn how to utter this word, which came out of the throat, the chest, the heart, the abdomen without being interrupted by lips or tongue or teeth. *Ai,* it was also the sound for a sigh when one was sad. A Chinese wouldn't know what *ai* meant until she or he had swallowed enough tears and bitterness.

I stretched my neck and sang as loudly as I could. I sang "Song of Four Seasons," starting with winter. I was finally able to fill in the blanks, to finish the song Mother had left me twenty years ago. It didn't matter what words I put into the song. The important thing was to keep trying. Mother had started all over again after Father died. She had learned the sword dance, fortune-telling, *taiqi* and *qigong*. Now she had so much *qi* in her body that she could cure the sick. At the age of 52, she had become a well known *qigong* master, traveling around China to heal the deaf and mute. As I sang, I made a decision: it was time to return to China again. I had two thousand dollars in my savings. Two hundred would be for my sister Sea Cloud, who had just married Zhang in Germany a week ago; two hundred for my youngest sister, Sea Gull, who was going to marry at the end of the year; one hundred for my brother, whose wife was expecting a baby; and one hundred for Waipo's eightieth birthday. After the plane fare, I would have only four hundred left for Mother. I wouldn't be able to buy her a piano. But again, the piano was not important. What mattered was my intention, my will to keep trying, always keep trying, no matter what.

COLOPHON

This book has been set in Spectrum and Carolus types with Adobe Wood Type dingbats. It has been printed at Friesen Printers, Altona, Manitoba, Canada, on Friesen Hi-bulk cream paper. As are all Coffee House Press books, this book has been smyth sewn for greater durability and ease of handling.